COMPACT YELLOWBILL
in association with TAMBARLE
presents a JOHN HOUGH film

starring
NEIL DICKSON
ALEX HYDE-WHITE
FIONA HUTCHISON
and PETER CUSHING as Colonel Raymond

Written by JOHN GROVES and KENT
WALWIN. Executive producer ADRIAN
SCROPE. Produced by POM OLIVER and
KENT WALWIN. Directed by
JOHN HOUGH.

**Also by the same author,
and available in Coronet Books:**

GHOSTBUSTERS

**Novelisation by
Larry Milne**

**Based on the screenplay
by John Groves and
Kent Walwin**

CORONET BOOKS
Hodder and Stoughton

Copyright © Yellowbill Services Limited
1985 and W. E. Johns (Publications) Limited
Novelisation copyright © 1986 by Larry Milne

First published in Great Britain in 1986
by Coronet Books

British Library C.I.P.

Milne, Larry
Biggles: the untold story
I. Title
823'.914[F]   PR6063.I378/
ISBN 0-340-38588-X

Printed and bound in Great Britain for
Hodder and Stoughton Paperbacks, a
division of Hodder and Stoughton Ltd.,
Mill Road, Dunton Green, Sevenoaks,
Kent (Editorial Office: 47 Bedford
Square, London, WC1 3DP) by
Cox and Wyman Ltd., Reading.
Photoset by Rowland Phototypesetting Ltd.,
Bury St Edmunds, Suffolk.

CONTENTS

1

THE STRANGER IN BLACK

A sudden squall of wind drove the last spatter of raindrops along the dark sidestreet in upper westside Manhattan, sweeping past the blank glass faces of the tall, anonymous apartment buildings. The late-evening thunderstorm had now abated, leaving a few faint rumbles as it receded distantly over the Hudson River towards New Jersey.

As the car turned the corner, its yellow headlights probing the darkness and smearing the slick-wet street with oily rainbows, the tall gaunt figure dressed all in black shrank deeper into the inky shadows of the brick archway.

It was time . . . This had to be him . . .

He waited and watched as the car pulled over to the kerb outside a smart modern block of concrete and glass with the name Lexington Apartments scrolled in stainless steel above the entrance. The man shifted his weight impatiently and flexed his gloved fingers.

At the wheel of the car, Debbie Stephens, pert and pretty and just twenty-one, glanced across at her passenger, who was at that moment stifling a yawn. She grinned good-naturedly.

'Home at last.'

Jim Ferguson grunted tiredly and reached for the door handle. 'Sure you won't come up? A little night-cap, maybe?'

Debbie waved a slender finger and gave him a look of admonishment with her large hazel eyes.

'You need to put your thinking cap on, mister,' she told him solemnly. 'You've still got the presentation to write. And anyway, it'll take me hours to sort all this stuff out.'

She gestured to the back of the car which was filled with posters and placards and stacks of aluminium foil dinner trays wrapped in plastic cling film. Tomorrow was the big day – the launch of their Celebrity TV Dinners enterprise. 'Eat with the Stars as you watch the Stars!' as their slogan proclaimed.

As partners in the new venture they'd worked long and hard to get this far. Invested time and money and all their hopes. For the moment their personal lives were on the back-burner.

Jim nodded and opened the door, zipping up his red windcheater against the cool night air. Debbie was right. There was still a heap of work to be done.

'See you tomorrow, Jim,' said Debbie fondly.

'Okay.' He leaned across to kiss her and then hopped out. The car moved off, headlights raking the brick archways on the opposite side of the street. Preoccupied and in a hurry, Debbie failed to notice the thin dark shape lurking there. But the man in the shadows had observed everything.

He glanced at the large pale face of his gold pocket watch and tucked it away, nodding slowly to himself.

Striding across the red terrazzo tiles fronting the

apartment building, Jim entered the glass-enclosed reception area. A tall, lithe young man with an athletic build, Jim Ferguson was the living model of the young entrepreneur. He had flair, initiative and hard-driving ambition – and at the moment he also had a lot on his plate. Two years of hard work and several hundred thousand dollars were riding on the launch of his brainchild tomorrow. And he still had that damn presentation speech to write.

As he vanished inside the building, the figure stepped out of the shadows and purposefully crossed the street.

A stray black cat, sheltering near the entrance, crouched back on its haunches at his approach, fur bristling, and then with a low howl scuttled off into the night.

The man stepped lightly across the tiled floor, an old-fashioned Homburg hat pulled down over his eyes and a black silk scarf swathing his chin, and pushed through the glass doors with a gloved hand.

Jim let himself into his apartment on the ninth floor. Mellow pools of light from the table-lamps transformed the L-shaped living-room, with its rough-cast walls and framed prints, into an oasis of comfort and solitude. Stretching his shoulders, he brushed both hands through his thick dark hair and debated for a moment whether to fix himself a drink, and then decided against it.

He needed a clear head right now; maybe later, as a small reward.

Settling himself on the couch, the slim silver micro-recorder in one hand, Jim prepared himself for creative thought. After fifteen seconds of staring into space and not a single creative thought in sight, he jumped up suddenly and began pacing up and down.

Come on now. This couldn't be all that hard. Ah . . . Ladies and gentlemen. Well, at least it was a start. Ladies and gentlemen, I would like to welcome you here today . . . er . . . my name is known to most of you . . . to some of you . . . my name is a mystery to all of you . . .

Jim frowned and stopped pacing as the lighting flickered. That was all he needed – a power cut. But after dimming a couple of times the lamps resumed their steady glow. Jim sat down again and pressed the tab to record. The little red light came on, glowing like a miniature ruby. He took a breath. Here goes . . .

'Ladies and Gentlemen, on behalf of Celebrity Dinners I would like to welcome you – '

There was a soft, insistent knock at the door.

Jim groaned and muttered a curse under his breath. Switching off the recorder, he dropped it on to the couch and traipsed to the door. His irritation turned to consternation. In the hallway, the dim light throwing into sharp relief his creased, hollow face and high cheekbones, stood a tall, erect figure who stared at him from under the curled brim of his hat. The man's eyes were a faded, dusty blue, but still keenly alert, almost piercing in their intensity.

'Yes?' Jim inquired politely, for a crazy moment imagining that the stranger had stepped out of another era, what with his immaculate dark clothes and refined, diffident manner.

Meeting only the same fixed stare, Jim tried again.

'Can I help you?'

The man moistened his lips. 'Are you James Ferguson?' he asked quietly. He spoke very carefully, in a precise English accent, as if weighing every word.

'Yes.' Jim narrowed his eyes a little. 'Who are you?'

The man blinked slowly, as if grappling unsuccessfully with a mental enigma wrapped in a paradox, and then leaned forward to peer closely into Jim's face. 'May I be so bold as to inquire,' he asked softly, 'if you are all right?'

'I'm fine,' Jim said, glancing down at himself. 'Why?'

The man sucked anxiously at his lower lip for a moment. Then, very concerned, he went on, 'Did something strange happen to you in the past few minutes?' He seemed to hold his breath, hanging on Jim's reply.

Jim shrugged. 'Nothing except you.' His irritation at being interrupted returned. It was late, he had work to do, and he was tired. 'Look – what do you want?'

'May I come in?'

'Not unless you can write a speech,' said Jim shortly. Who the hell *was* this guy? He said, 'No, I'm sorry, I'm very busy right now,' and started to close the door.

The man in black fumbled inside his overcoat. 'Do you have the correct time?' he asked, frowning down at the gold pocket watch in the soft leather palm of his glove.

Jim sighed and glanced at his watch.

'It's eleven-sixteen exactly.'

'Eleven-sixteen exactly,' the man repeated in a hoarse whisper. The faded blue of his eyes seemed to glaze over. His lips moved numbly. 'It must be a mistake. It should have happened by now.'

Jim decided to humour him. 'Yes, of course it should,' he agreed with a tight smile. He gripped the edge of the door.

'Look, I'm very busy. I don't know what the hell you're talking about, so if you'll excuse me I've got to go.'

'I'm sorry to have troubled you . . . Mr Ferguson.' The elderly man backed away into the gloom of the hallway, his narrow creased face displaying a kind of blank bafflement. 'Goodnight . . .'

Thankfully, Jim shut the door, shaking his head. No doubt about it, New York was definitely deteriorating.

'Weirdo,' he murmured under his breath, returning to the couch and picking up the recorder. Maybe this time he could get through it in one shot, he hoped, standing in the centre of the room and struggling to gather his scattered thoughts.

He thumbed the tab.

'Ladies and gentlemen. My name is Jim Ferguson. Welcome to Celebrity Dinners – '

The rest of the sentence seized up in his throat as Jim found himself staring goggle-eyed at the hand holding the recorder. Blue electric sparks were shimmering between his fingertips. He yelped as they spread quickly down his arm and enveloped his whole body in a dazzling blue force-field of quantum energy.

What the hell – ?

Then the table-lamps started to flash on and off erratically, shadows flickering and darting across the ceiling. Suddenly they went out, plunging the room into total darkness. A fierce wind sprang up from nowhere, ruffling Jim's hair to an icy blast, and involuntarily he staggered forward and felt something cold and wet seeping straight through his shoe and sock and chilling him to the bone.

Jim looked down, and in the dim, eerie light saw that he was standing ankle-deep in a puddle of freezing mud and icy water.

* * *

Jim raised his head and gazed around him, slack-jawed.

Instead of his warm, friendly apartment he was now confronted by a hellish lunar landscape of frozen mud and black gaping craters under a pale slice of crescent moon. A cold wind blew relentlessly across the bleak terrain, making him shiver. On the jagged horizon, shattered and splintered trees leaned at weary angles, starkly outlined against the dark rolling clouds.

Jim dragged at his foot and it came away with a glutinous sucking sound. As he did so, he heard another, more fearful sound in the far distance – the sharp, metallic rattle of a machine-gun. Immediately it was answered by the drilling clatter of another gun, this time nearer – much nearer. And beyond the splintered trees on the broken horizon, the sky was instantly illuminated by a bright blinding flash followed moments later by the gritty crunch of the explosion as the shock-wave reached him.

Shrapnel rained down. Jim cowered and shielded his head. From under his raised arms he stared out at this scene of terrible devastation. He wasn't drunk, so what was this – nightmare? Hallucination? Whatever it was he didn't much like it. Not one bit. It was too damn real.

A shadow passed across the moon. Jim squinted up and through the darkness made out the darker solid shape of an aircraft – an old World War I biplane, staggering at zero feet over the churned-up cratered landscape towards him, its engine spluttering raggedly and coughing like a rusty tractor.

For perhaps five seconds, or several lifetimes, Jim stood rooted to the spot. If this was another hallucination it was earsplittingly loud, looked all too real, and was heading straight for him.

At the last moment Jim came to the rapid conclusion that it was real enough for him, and dived full-length. He hit the muddy ground with a bone-jarring thud as the biplane, the fabric of its wings flapping in rags and tatters, passed directly over his head, its engine stuttering and missing. Ten yards further on the tubular-braced undercarriage crumpled as it struck a mound of earth, the left wingtip tilted and ploughed a deep furrow, and the aircraft reared up on its nose and pitched over on to its back with an horrendous crash of breaking timber and tortured metal.

There it lay, mangled and still, like a broken bird.

Jim was on his feet and running before he realised it. Slithering and sliding through the mud, he got to the machine and ducked under the main wing. A dull smoky flame sprang up and flickered behind the engine cowling. The sharp reek of petroleum vapour stung his nostrils.

Hanging upside down, still strapped inside the

cockpit, the goggled and leather-helmeted pilot was struggling to free himself.

It was even money which of the two of them was the most astonished by the confrontation; had he been the right way up, the pilot's jaw might have dropped at the sight of Jim, dressed in his red zippered windcheater, appearing from nowhere.

As it was, he had other things on his mind.

'Lend a hand, I'm in a bit of a pinch here, old man,' the pilot called out, sounding remarkably cheerful under the circumstances. 'Something very strange just happened to my plane.'

'You're not kidding,' Jim mumbled. From the pilot's accent he supposed that this was a piece of typical British understatement.

Apparently the stiff upper lip was alive and well in whatever nightmare Jim had happened to fall into.

'Hurry it along, will you, old chap?' said the pilot, a mite peeved. 'They'll start to whizz-bang us in a moment.' He grunted between gritted teeth. 'Bloody harness is stuck . . .'

'What the hell is going on?'

'No time for speculation,' said the pilot crisply. 'Step lively now!'

Jim dropped to his knees and tugged at the straps, managing to get one shoulder free. In the midst of his struggles the pilot suddenly went still, listening. Jim listened too. There came a dull boom somewhere beyond the horizon, like a heavy door closing deep in a cellar, then a faint shrieking whistle that got louder and louder, and then a deafening WHOOMPH! as the mortar shell landed not twenty feet away, throwing up a column of earth and frozen mud. Clods of earth and stones rattled over the wings and fuselage.

Jim winced and rubbed his forehead where he had been struck.

'Was that for real?' he asked incredulously – knowing the question to be superfluous as he felt the slow warm trickle of blood on his right temple.

The pilot laughed softly. 'Good old Fritz,' he murmured, half to himself. 'His first two always miss.'

Jim redoubled his efforts with the harness and in a moment or two the pilot, by twisting sideways and heaving on Jim's arm, was able to squirm free, and tumbled to the ground.

Once again they heard the dull boom of the trench mortar, followed by the thin rising whine of the shell's trajectory. This time the aim was better – rather too close for comfort, Jim felt – as the shell exploded less than ten feet away, on the far side of the aircraft.

'Come on!' snapped the pilot grimly, crawling out and heaving himself upright. He grabbed Jim by the arm and propelled him forward, and together they staggered through the waterlogged shell-holes and thick clinging mud. They hadn't gone more than a dozen paces when once again the dull distant thud of the cellar door boomed across the blasted landscape, and Jim was sent sprawling by a tremendous shove in the back. Winded by the fall, lying in a pool of black icy water, he heard the by now familiar shriek of the incoming projectile, and a split-second later there was a blinding flash and ear-splitting $c - r - u - n - c - h$ as the shell scored a direct hit on the biplane.

The flimsy aircraft disintegrated in a whirling orange fireball which spiralled into the dark scudding

16

sky, carrying with it flaming scraps of fabric and charred splinters of plywood. Dense oily smoke rose up from the burning wreckage, like a thick twisting rope.

Numb with shock, frozen to the marrow, his ears still ringing from the blast of the explosion, Jim slowly sat up and looked dazedly around him. The pilot had scrambled to his feet and was gazing gloomily at what was left of his plane.

'Damn,' he muttered through clenched teeth to no one in particular. 'Lost the bloody photographs.'

He tugged off his flying helmet and goggles and pushed his hand through his short dark hair. 'Stuck my backside in a grinder to get them. Now I'll have to go out tomorrow and do it again.'

He swung round and offered a helping hand as Jim struggled wearily to climb out of the mud. In the flickering ruddy glow from the burning plane, Jim got his first proper look at him. He was a young, clean-shaven man with a keen, intelligent face and shrewd, watchful eyes not without a twinkle of humour residing in their grey depths. He was roughly the same height as Jim, though broader and more powerfully built, wearing the type of period flying kit Jim had seen in old photographs and movies: fur-lined leather jacket and gauntlets, tight-fitting jodhpurs, and stout lace-up leather boots. A white scarf, loosely furled round his neck, trailed negligently over one shoulder.

The outmoded phrase, *a gentleman of the old school*, flitted through Jim's mind, which seemed to fit his new companion like a glove.

The pilot grinned and thrust out his hand.

'Thanks for your help,' he said genially. 'Don't

think we've been properly introduced. I'm James Bigglesworth. My friends call me Biggles.'

They shook hands and Jim said woodenly, 'Jim Ferguson. Celebrity Dinners,' and automatically felt in his pocket for his business card.

Biggles took the proffered card and bent closer to study it. His face cleared and he raised his eyebrows in mild surprise.

'I say! You're an American! I heard you chaps were coming over.' He eyed Jim's windcheater critically. 'Uniforms on the way, I suppose.'

Jim opened his mouth, intending to ask this Biggles guy what the hell was going on and what was he, Jim, doing out here in the middle of a battlefield? But he was cut short by the sudden vicious rattle of a machine-gun opening up nearby.

Then all hell broke loose as the sky became alive with tracers streaking overhead, bullets zinging past his ear, and once again the ominous dull thudding boom of the trench mortars.

Instinctively, Biggles ducked and grabbed Jim's arm, pulling him down.

'The Huns have a fix on us,' he said tersely. 'We'd best get back to our own side.' He glanced up, his square jaw set determinedly, a muscle rippling in his cheek.

'Come on!'

He jerked his head towards the broken line of the horizon with its shattered, stunted trees and set off in a low, crouching run.

Jim started to follow and then stopped. This was ridiculous! He straightened up, hands on hips, and shook his head in mute wonder. 'What am I *doing* here?' he muttered to himself. 'What's going on? Where the hell am I?'

Biggles had turned and was gesturing with his gloved hand. Jim shrugged at him and spread his arms.

'Oh no . . . Oh God!'

Jim stared at his hands. They were outlined with a pale yellowish glow, a kind of fuzzy dancing halo. Sparks jumped between his fingertips.

The first of the mortar shells exploding thirty feet away brought him back to his senses. The second came in, whining like a banshee, and threw up a great gout of earth and mud that showered down all around him.

Jim tensed. He braced himself. He didn't believe in any of this, but he wasn't going to get himself killed proving it.

With a hideous screeching howl the third mortar zoomed towards him, dead on target, and Jim leapt for his life.

* * *

But he was in for another shock.

Instead of landing at the bottom of a shell-hole he crashed into something soft and springy, bounced off again and hit something hard and solid with a thud that jarred his backbone.

Jim opened his eyes dazedly and looked around. He was lying on the carpet next to the couch.

His carpet next to his couch in his apartment.

. . . no exploding mortar shells, no chattering machine-guns, no burning aircraft, no pitted battle-field . . .

Everything normal, safe, quiet.

Jim gave a huge sigh of heartfelt relief. It had all been a stupid crazy dream, all in his imagination. He'd been overworking. He was tired and overwrought, that was it. Of course. Had to be.

This was what he told himself – and almost convinced himself – until he tried to get groggily to his feet and found that he ached from head to foot. Worst of all, when he touched his forehead his fingers came away sticky with blood.

Jim looked down at himself, at his wet and mud-stained windcheater, at his pants dripping water on to the carpet, and at his shoes, covered in thick, black, clinging mud.

2

A VISIT FROM THE COLONEL

Bill Kizitski stared with bulging eyes at the plastic tray lid that his secretary, Judy, had a moment ago placed on his desk. He squeezed his eyes shut and opened them again, but the offending picture on the label, in glorious full colour and unexpurgated detail, was still there.

The executive marketing director of Celebrity Dinners covered his mouth with his hand, fingers digging into the thick dark undergrowth of his beard, and moaned with a mixture of rage and despair. After all their sweat and effort, the months of careful preparation and planning, all that *work* – and look what that moron had gone and done!

Snatching up the lid, Bill stormed angrily into the main office and glared balefully around him. A cardboard mountain of packing cartons had been erected in the centre of the carpeted, open-plan area, and there – delving into an open carton – was the object of Bill's wrath and the bane of his life, Chuck Dinsmore, 225 pounds of pale blubber in a tight-fitting business suit, his several chins cascading over his button-down collar and floral tie.

'Chuck! Goddammit!' yelled Bill, charging forward.

Chuck Dinsmore glanced up, clutching a stack of tray lids, his round face wreathed in a fat, triumphant smile. 'Hey, Bill, have you seen the tray lids? They look great!'

Bill stood before him, eyes hooded with anger, and said in a low, furious voice, 'You were supposed to feature a typical American family – mom, dad, a boy of twelve and a girl of ten . . .'

Chuck nodded eagerly. 'That's what you got!'

Bill strode across to a large placard, eight feet by four, propped against a desk. A life-size blow-up of the picture on the tray lid, it showed a 'typical American family' sitting cosily round their TV set.

Except for the little girl who was blonde, voluptuous, not a day under eighteen, and who wouldn't have disgraced a *Playboy* centre-spread.

'That's a girl of *ten*?' Bill squeaked, rapping the placard where the girl's breasts swelled dangerously over her tank top, threatening to escape.

'So, she's a little – ' Chuck waggled his fat paws and shrugged ' – prematurely developed,' he conceded.

Bill swallowed hard and raised a trembling finger.

'We spent sixteen thousand dollars to get a profile of the typical American family, based on market surveys and buyers' polls – '

Chuck wasn't impressed. 'Hey, listen, Mister Marketing Expert,' he retorted sarcastically. 'You don't need a survey to know that *tits sell*!' He beamed smugly.

Bill clenched both fists and was actually considering something violent and possibly terminal when he spotted Jim entering through reception. With immense relief he turned away and hurried to meet him.

Having spent the past forty minutes trying to control her mounting impatience at Jim's non-arrival, Debbie was on the lookout and beat Bill Kizitski to it. She couldn't understand how Jim could be late, especially on this, the most important day of their business lives. It just wasn't like him – not with the product launch only hours away.

She thrust the clipboard under Jim's nose, coolly flicking back a stray curl of her rich auburn hair.

'I need to run through the final cost-unit figures with you,' she began tartly, before noticing the band-aid on the side of his forehead. 'What happened to your head?' she inquired, immediately concerned.

'Bumped into a door; it's nothing. Sorry I'm late.'

His face was rather pale, Debbie now realised. His manner was abrupt and he seemed edgy and distracted.

'This is ridiculous!' Bill had seized Jim firmly by the arm and was leading the young man over to the placard. 'We can't let the buyers see this, Jim,' he protested, gesturing at the photograph with obvious disgust. 'Look at that girl's breasts. You moron!' he added for Chuck's benefit, who was standing there quite unconcerned, twiddling his fat thumbs.

Jim looked at it – or rather, them – and cringed.

He looked wordlessly at Chuck.

Chuck folded his arms. 'Jim, we need this cover,' he insisted calmly. 'It's modern, it's stylish, it's sexy.' Warming to his theme, he went on, 'It's what Young America is all about today. Tits and TV!'

'Maybe you're right,' said Jim slowly. He shook his head. 'But this just isn't us.'

Chuck frowned in disappointment and Bill sighed with relief. But a problem still remained, as Bill was quick to point out.

'It's too late to get new ones made before this afternoon,' he said, anxiously gnawing a thumb-nail.

Jim straightened his shoulders and seemed to snap out of his trance. Decisively, he tapped out the points on his fingers.

'Okay, here's what we'll do. Bill: only put the lids on a few of the trays and put them on separate tables – like we're trying to get a sample reaction. Then – use something to cover up the girl. A label or a strip of ad copy or something. Tell the buyers we haven't made a final decision on the cover yet.'

'Right,' Bill said gratefully. He bustled off, shooting a final poisonous glare at Chuck.

Jim went over to inspect the open trays of food, laid out in rows on a table by the window. He looked critically at a TV chicken dinner, complete with apple sauce, potatoes and sweet corn, and nodded to himself, satisfied.

'Looks almost good enough to eat, hey?' said Chuck, trailing up behind, appraising the food with a professional glutton's greedy eye.

His hand hovered over a drumstick, and while Jim's back was turned he took a swift bite and popped it back on the tray. He chewed and gulped it down behind a raised hand as Jim glanced up at him and smiled.

'It all looks fantastic.'

On his way to his office Jim was waylaid by Bill, still quietly fuming.

'When are we gonna dump that big pile of shit?' demanded the marketing director through his teeth.

Jim sighed and said patiently, 'Chuck has some good ideas . . . and as long as his uncle runs the bank that gave us our loan, he's married to us.' He patted Bill's shoulder. 'Try to get along with him, okay?'

Debbie was waiting for Jim in his office. He gave her a weary smile. 'Look, please try and control Chuck, if only for today.'

'Okay, but I can't do everything.' Debbie frowned, seeing the lines of strain round his mouth. 'Look, Jim, it's the big day . . . after two horrible years of blood, sweat and meatballs we're almost there.'

'Today New York,' said Jim lightly. 'Tomorrow Kansas City and Kalamazoo . . .'

His voice trailed away. His lean, tanned face visibly paled.

Through the glass partition he had glimpsed a tall gaunt figure dressed in black moving past reception and heading directly towards his office. Jim came quickly round the desk and took Debbie by the elbow. 'Let's take a break. Give me a moment to deal with this guy.' He jerked his head.

'We really need to go through this, Jim,' Debbie protested, holding up the clipboard.

'I'll just be a minute, I promise,' Jim insisted, pushing her gently but firmly to the door.

Debbie shrugged and went out, glancing back curiously as the elderly, distinguished stranger with the piercing blue eyes and erect, military bearing entered the office.

Jim closed the door and turned to face his visitor, who was regarding him with a keen, searching look. He was dressed as on the previous evening, in a long dark overcoat, black silk scarf, and black Homburg, its narrow brim and crown emphasising even more the hollow, sharply etched features and high cheek-bones.

Jim tapped his wrist. 'It's now 9.30. In three hours it'll be 12.30, at which time I have a very important job to do – '

'I see that you hurt your head,' murmured the man gently. He raised his eyebrows as Jim's hand automatically went to the band-aid. 'Did it happen last night?' he inquired in the same calm, evenly modulated tone.

'What is this – twenty questions?'

'Did you knock your head on a burning plane?'

Jim went very still. A muscle twitched in his cheek. 'Now why do you say that?' he asked in a low voice.

'Did you rescue the pilot?' the other went on in his quiet, remorseless manner.

There was a silence during which Jim stared at the man. He took a breath and moistened his lips. 'Who the hell are you?'

'Then it did happen last night,' the man said, nodding slowly, speaking as if to himself.

He took a card from his inside pocket and held it out with a faint smile.

As Jim studied it the man leaned forward and pressed the fingertips of his black gloves together. A new hard light entered his eyes and his voice gained a sharper edge of urgency.

'You must tell me. It's important that you tell me *exactly* what happened . . .'

'Colonel Raymond. Special Air Intelligence.' Jim looked up from the card, his eyes narrowing. 'What is this? Are you investigating me?'

'No, no, nothing like that . . . but please go on. You must tell me.'

Jim sat on the corner of the desk and stroked the band-aid with thoughtful fingers. After a moment of lingering indecision, he said quietly, 'Okay. I was trying to write a speech in my living-room. You knocked at my door and asked me what time it was. Then you went away. I heard a lot of thunder, sparks were flashing, and there was a wind blowing through my apartment . . .'

He looked up with a vague frown, his dark eyes mirroring his inner confusion. 'The next thing I know, I'm in the middle of some big battle somewhere . . .'

'The Western Front, 1917.'

'How do you know that?'

'Please go on,' pressed Colonel Raymond in his gentle, precise tones.

'. . . A plane crashed,' Jim said slowly, remembering. 'An old biplane. I helped the pilot get out. He had a funny name – Bigglesburg or something.'

'You rescued him?' The colonel was watching him with an almost hypnotic intensity, hanging on every word. 'You rescued Biggles?'

'That's right. Biggles. Anyway,' Jim continued, 'there was a lot of shooting and bombing and the plane blew up. Next thing I know I was back in my apartment again.' He wagged his head to and fro. 'Jesus, it sounds so crazy!'

'What about the camera?' asked Colonel Raymond sharply.

'Camera?'

'The camera on the aircraft. Did Biggles retrieve it?'

Jim thought for a bit, and then shrugged. 'I don't remember.'

'Try. *Please try*.'

'Wait.' Jim closed his eyes and massaged his temple. Gradually it came back, like fragments from a dream. 'That's right. Biggles said he had to get his camera. But we never made it.'

Colonel Raymond stared at him. 'You mean you *didn't* get the camera?' he asked in a whisper.

'No. The plane blew up before there was time.'

Raymond's lean figure turned away, his gloved hands clenching and unclenching. His face seemed to have been pulled taut, its deeply etched lines frozen into a bleak mask.

Jim caught a muttered, 'This is very awkward' – again as if the man was speaking to himself.

'Listen, Mr Raymond, or whoever you are,' Jim said, sliding off the desk and standing up. 'Would you please tell me what's going on? I think at the very least . . .'

There was a brief rap on the door and Bill Kizitski stuck his bearded head in. 'Jim, we've got a glitch in the mashed potatoes – '

'Just a minute, Bill, okay?' Jim snapped, glaring at him.

Bill retired as if bitten and quickly closed the door, wearing a hurt look.

Jim turned back to Colonel Raymond, who was buttoning his overcoat.

'If something else should happen to you, you must come to London at once,' the colonel told him brusquely, already halfway to the door.

'London! Are you crazy?'

The colonel paused in the doorway.

'My address is on the card,' he said, turned on his heel and strode out through reception, Jim following in his wake.

As Colonel Raymond vanished through the doors, Jim halted in the middle of the floor, suddenly aware that the bustle of activity had ceased and that he was the target of all eyes.

He swivelled round, hands on hips, angry and baffled and embarrassed, and barked out, 'Well? Is everybody taking the day off? We've got a presentation in three hours!'

Fingering the piece of card, he thoughtfully returned to his office and closed the door.

3

BIGGLES GOES ON A RECCE

Thank goodness! All the important out-of-town buyers had shown up, Debbie saw with relief, looking round the crowded hotel banqueting suite they had hired for the launch.

Covertly, she adjusted the low neckline of her glittering red diamante gown on her slender shoulders, smoothing the material where it clung to her waist and hips like a second skin. For the occasion she had swept her long auburn hair up on to her head in a rich glowing coil. She felt cool and poised and ready for the fray.

And so far – fingers crossed – everything seemed to be going according to plan. Bill and his marketing people had set up an impressive display of publicity material, with giant-sized stills of Linda Evans, Joan Collins, Arnold Schwarzenegger and other TV and movie stars, promoting the theme of TV dinners of superstar quality. Spotlit tables covered in crisp white linen were arranged at strategic intervals, each with a selection of dinners. Stunning girls wearing gold CELEBRITY DINNER sashes ghosted lithely to and fro, dispensing drinks.

Even the offending placard had been taken care of: a label reading 'INTRODUCTORY LOW PRICE' had been pasted over the young lady's amply developed chest. Once again, Jim's quick thinking had saved the day.

Debbie frowned slightly as she caught sight of Chuck holding a young and attractive female buyer in intimate discourse. A leering smile had lodged itself on his round, perspiring face. She would have to keep an eye on old Chuck, in case his lecherous ways lost them friends, not to mention several hundred thousands dollars' worth of orders.

'How's it going?'

Jim's appearance took her breath away a little. He looked very handsome in bow tie, frilled shirt and immaculate white tuxedo, smiling down at her with a rather nervous, boyish air.

She stood on tip-toe and kissed the dimple on his chin.

'Okay so far,' Debbie informed him brightly. 'The buyer from National Markets just arrived.'

Jim squared his shoulders resolutely, then had a last-second panic. 'My tie okay? My head on?' He cleared his throat. 'Wish me luck.'

Debbie pursed her lips. 'You'll need it. It's Maxine Fine.'

'Oh Jeez . . .' Jim winced. Then he shrugged philosophically. Well, start with the tough ones and work downwards.

They didn't come much tougher than Maxine Fine. Jim summoned up his friendliest smile and most confident, cordial manner and approached the tall, elegant black woman who was peering somewhat dubiously at the open trays of food laid before her.

'Hello, Mrs Fine! Nice to see you. Thanks for coming.'

Maxine Fine graciously extended her hand and Jim shook it warmly.

'Hello, Ferguson,' she answered, appraising him coolly, and tilted her coiffured head to indicate the thronged room under the glittering chandeliers. 'So this is it, huh? Breaking into the big time.'

'I think we've got the product to do it,' said Jim modestly.

Maxine Fine arched one eyebrow. 'We'll see.'

'Here – ' Jim reached for one of the steaming trays and held it out for her inspection. As she accepted it Jim's hand twitched. He sneaked a glance at the ceiling. Was that thunder, or had he imagined it?

He switched his attention back to Maxine Fine. Who, as bad luck would have it, had noticed one of the undoctored tray lids showing the typical American family and Chuck's idea of a ten-year-old girl. Mrs Fine was not amused.

'What are you selling here?' she asked laconically. 'Silicone implants?'

'Oh, you mean the cover?' Jim laughed merrily. 'Just trying it out . . . market research.' Quickly he turned the lid face down. 'We're replacing it with a new one.'

Maxine Fine gave him a disapproving look and dipped her head into the tray, sniffing audibly. 'Not much nose,' she pronounced curtly. 'Consumers want a lot of nose in their dinners.'

Jim was anxious to reassure her. 'We can certainly improve on that – ' He broke off and hunched his shoulders instinctively as a long, low rumble of thunder rolled across the heavens. No doubt about it that time.

'Could mean rain,' remarked Maxine Fine offhandedly, looking towards the grey city panorama through the picture window.

It could mean something else too, Jim thought desperately, fearing the worst. Get a grip, Ferguson, he told himself, fingernails digging into his palms. Nothing's going to happen. Everything is Perfectly Normal. Including me.

With an effort he brought his mind back to the business in hand, watching Mrs Fine pick up a chicken drumstick and bare strong white teeth as she prepared to take a bite. In horror, Jim saw that somebody had beaten her to it. He could even see the teeth marks.

She saw it too and stared in disbelief. 'What the hell . . .?'

'I'm very sorry, let me get you another dinner.'

Jim hurriedly took the drumstick and tray from her, looking round for Chuck from under thunderous lowered brows; but Chuck had witnessed the minor commotion and was hiding his bulk as best he could behind the largest rubber plant he could find.

Maxine Fine waved her hand. 'That's okay. At least somebody wanted to eat it. I'm not sure about that corn though,' she said with a grimace. 'It looks a little like dog puke.'

Jim took a fork and with an elaborate gesture scooped up some corn and chewed it with obvious relish, like a connoisseur tasting the best caviar.

'Mrs Fine – your customers will tell you that this is the finest dog puke they've ever tasted!'

Maxine Fine threw back her head and laughed. Jim

laughed with her. His laughter became hollow as lightning streaked jaggedly outside the window. And then – directly overhead – there came a tremendous crash of thunder that shook the room. The buzz of conversation died as the lighting dimmed, everyone looking up at the chandeliers.

Everyone, that is, except Jim. He had dropped the tray and was trying to back away from the blue sparks arcing between his splayed fingertips.

The room's lighting resumed its normal brightness. The chatter started up again. Jim edged away from the table, staring at his hands as if they might leap up and throttle him. With a mumbled, 'Excuse me for a moment,' he turned and bolted for the exit, but never got that far. With every step the vivid blue force-field seemed to intensify. Jim tried to run away from it but couldn't. Sparks were jumping from his shoes. His entire body was alive with the powerful and mysterious aura of glowing plasma.

There was nowhere to go, nowhere to hide.

In desperation and panic, Jim leapt out of sight behind a life-size blow-up of Arnold Schwarzenegger flexing his oiled biceps. There he crouched, holding his head in his arms. He shivered. It had suddenly gone cold.

Very cold.

Freezing.

* * *

Jim cautiously opened his eyes. He blinked them shut and then slowly and reluctantly opened them again.

There was no mistake. Still wearing his white tuxedo and black bow-tie, he was sitting in the open rear cockpit of a biplane which was standing on a wind-swept snow-covered airfield somewhere in the past. A past that Colonel Raymond had told him was the Western Front, 1917.

A bulky figure, swaddled in a well-worn flying jacket with a fur collar, and swathed in a thick white woollen scarf, wearing a leather helmet and goggles, climbed onto the wing. The left shoulder of his leather coat was stained with a dark patch, the residue of hot castor oil flung out of the cylinder heads of the rotary engine. Camel pilots were instantly recognisable by the dark stain and the sweet, sickly smell of castor oil that hung about them.

Biggles swung round, eyes wide and startled.

'You again! What the deuce are you doing in my plane?'

'I'm not sure,' said Jim lamely.

In the crisp wintry light the young British flyer's face bore the marks of strain and fatigue: finely etched lines round the corners of his eyes and mouth. But the grey eyes themselves were clear and steady, with a cool authority and self-confidence beyond his years.

'You've been assigned to the wrong plane,' declared Biggles, clambering into the forward cockpit and fastening his Sutton harness. He added grimly, 'This may be a one-way mission.'

Swiftly checking the primitive instrument panel, with its altimeter, inclinometer and rev-counter, he stuck out an arm and gave the thumbs-up to the mechanic holding the single-blade wooden prop.

'What do you mean – one way?' asked Jim, dry-mouthed.

'The Germans have a new weapon, the one that caused me to crash. I'm going to try and take another photograph.' Biggles jabbed his finger to indicate a large square varnished box mounted on the leading edge of the lower wing. A rubber tube snaked from the box into the cockpit. 'They may try to use the weapon against us.'

Biggles craned his neck and gave Jim a cheery grin. 'Now that you're here, make yourself useful. There's a helmet in the cockpit. Keep a lookout.'

Jim half-rose in his seat. 'Biggles, I have to talk to you!'

His shouted plea was almost drowned as the mechanic swung the propeller and the 110-horsepower Clerget rotary engine fired explosively and roared into vibrant life, the struts, wires and fabric-covered wings trembling like something alive.

Jim sat down again quickly and started buckling the straps.

'Don't talk – look!' Biggles shouted, pulling down his goggles. He kicked on top rudder to bring the Sopwith Strutter round into the wind, and the aircraft trundled forward over the bumpy, snow-covered ground on its large solid rubber-rimmed wheels.

'Look for what?' asked Jim plaintively, gazing all around.

But his words were snatched away in the slipstream as Biggles opened the throttle and the machine surged forward, sending up a billowing cloud of snow, and sailed gracefully into the gloomy leaden sky.

* * *

A few snowflakes were drifting down on another airfield, not many miles away on the other side of the German lines, as the armoured half-track rattled to a halt on the edge of the landing strip.

From it stepped a tall, erect figure wearing a tightly buttoned greatcoat and black boots polished to gleaming perfection. On his breast he sported the pearl-grey wings with white markings of the *Jagdstaffeln* – the dreaded hunter squadrons of fast interceptor fighters of the German High Command. Under the peaked cap the lean face was hard and brutal, complemented by icy blue eyes and a thin mouth with a sardonic twist to it.

Hauptmann Erich von Stalhein strode across to the waiting Fokker Dr-1, painted all in black except for the aluminium cowling, its engine idling, and swung himself into the cockpit.

Handing his cap to a corporal, von Stalhein took the rivetted iron mask and fitted it over his close-cropped head, clicking the slitted visor into place.

The aircraft taxied forward and turned into the wind, the whirling arc of the propeller flashing like a pale silver coin in the drab light. Moments later it was climbing steeply and banking to the east, the black Iron Crosses outlined in white on wings and fuselage soon obscured by the thickening, billowing flakes.

`       *    *    *`

Biggles leaned over the side of the cockpit, eyes scanning the battle-scarred ground below like a hawk. In his gloved hand he held a black rubber bulb which triggered the camera mechanism.

Huddled inside the unheated cockpit, dressed in his white dinner jacket, black bow-tie and thin frilly shirt, Jim was slowly freezing to death. Between him and the vicious backlash of air from the propeller was only a tiny angled windscreen, no bigger than a pocket handkerchief.

He still hadn't a clue what Biggles was searching for, but it had better be damn well worth it – whatever *it* was.

At less than a thousand feet they flew on over the ravaged pock-marked countryside, heading deeper behind the German lines.

Biggles kept his eyes peeled for 'Archie' – the pilots' term for the puffs of black smoke that indicated enemy anti-aircraft fire – but thankfully saw none. Periodically he squinted between outstretched gloved fingers at the white blur of the sun, searching for signs of enemy scouts, but again the sky remained mercifully empty.

Still, Biggles fretted a little and wished he was flying his Camel. The Sopwith Strutter wasn't a bad machine as a range-finder for the artillery, and for reconnaisance duties such as this, but it was clumsy and slow compared to the Camel's turn of speed and wonderful lightning manoeuvrability. Some Camel pilots called it 'the vicious little beast' because of its unnerving trait, due to the engine's torque effect, of pulling sharply to the right, which, if uncorrected, was liable to finish in a fatal spin. Indeed, some novice pilots had crashed on take-off, before getting thirty feet off the ground.

But this same characteristic, in experienced hands, allowed the Camel to perform lightning flick rolls, giving it an amazing agility in a dog-fight that the Fokkers and Albatros D–IIIs couldn't match. Yes, he'd have felt a lot happier in his Camel, Biggles reflected, especially if they happened to run across a German 'circus'.

A vee-formation of British DH4s passed above them, returning from a patrol, the observers leaning against their gun-rings and waving a greeting, which Biggles returned.

Numbed by the cold and the endlessly droning engine, Jim's thoughts were aimless, his senses befuddled. With Biggles intent on watching the ground, the first whiff of danger either of them had was a distant clatter, like pebbles on a corrugated roof.

Jim spun round in his seat. 'There's somebody on our tail!' he yelled at the top of his voice.

Hardly had he spoken when a vicious spray of tracer bullets drilled a row of ragged holes through the fabric, right under his nose, hitting with a flat, angry *thwack–thwack–thwack–thwack*.

Jim's entire arm was wrenched forward. Looking down, he stared in disbelief at the gaping gash in his sleeve, just below the shoulder, where the bullet had passed clean through.

Within seconds of the attack, Biggles had taken swift evasive action. Throttling back almost to a stall and holding the joystick full over to the right, he flung the Sopwith into a near vertical side-slip, hurtling towards the earth in an attempt to shake off their pursuer. The wings quivered under the tremendous strain, the taut wires shrieking in the blast of air. At the last possible moment, a mere hundred or so feet above the ground, he opened the throttle wide, kicked hard on left rudder, and hauled the machine upwards in a screaming climb that strained the airframe to its limit.

Levelling out, Biggles raked the sky for their attacker, and spotted it at once on their left rear quarter. The all-black Fokker with the aluminium cowling was banking sharply, lining up for a second attack. Biggles tightened his jaw. This was an old adversary, one he had crossed swords with before.

His old duelling partner – the man in the iron mask.

Biggles ground his teeth in frustration at being caught in the slower and more cumbersome Strutter. It wasn't just the Camel's speed and manoeuvrability he yearned for: its armament was superior to anything the Huns could muster – a formidable pair of side-by-side synchronised Vickers giving maximum rate-of-fire through the airscrew of 300 rounds per minute.

However, no good wishing for the moon, thought Biggles grimly. Top priority was to get out of this fix first.

'Get ready to fight,' he shouted out to Jim. 'Check the gun.'

Jim goggled at him. Until now he hadn't paid any attention to the wide-nozzled Lewis gun with its round magazine drum, pillar-mounted on a greased ring behind his head.

'I don't know how to fire it!'

'What the hell did they teach you in training school?' demanded Biggles hotly.

'Cooking.'

The Fokker was above them, using its superior height to make its attack. As the twin Spandau guns started blazing through the swirling arc of the propeller-blade, Biggles squirmed round in his seat and yelled at Jim, 'Shoot back at the blighter!'

Kneeling up in the cramped plywood seat, Jim grabbed the double handgrip, gritted his teeth, and pulled the trigger. The noise and hammering recoil were horrendous. Jim thought his brain was falling apart. Pelted with hot shell casings, he blasted away indiscriminately for all he was worth in the general direction of the diving aircraft, the pilot's iron mask clearly visible between the spitting guns.

After a bit of a struggle, Jim managed to master the juddering beast and was now aiming with greater accuracy. But just when he thought he had the German aircraft in his sights the pilot flung his flimsy machine into an incredible tight turn, swooping low and vanishing under the Sopwith's tailplane.

Jim swung the heavy Lewis gun round on its greased ring, ready for a new angle of attack. It never came. Instead, the Fokker was climbing steeply away from them, heading eastward – evidently breaking off the aerial engagement.

With puzzled eyes, Biggles gazed through the windscreen at the disappearing German fighter. 'That's very odd,' he muttered to himself, frowning.

Deciding to keep the aircraft in view, he increased the revs and lifted the nose, seeking to gain height. For some time he climbed steadily, watching his air-speed indicator and revolutions counter closely.

At about four thousand feet, with the Fokker now a distant speck against the banks of dark cloud, Biggles saw something that brought a low whistle to his lips. A thin line of smoke arced from the aircraft, ending in a brilliant blue flare which seemed to hang for ages against the grey backdrop of sky.

Obviously a signal to somebody on the ground, Biggles surmised, but who – and more importantly, why? What game was the pilot in the iron mask playing?

The flare sputtered and died and spiralled to the ground, leaving a smoky trail. Using this as a guide, Biggles pushed the stick forward and followed it down. The terrain beneath had changed from the scarred battlefield of frozen mud to a gentle rolling patchwork of fields, hedgerows and groves of trees. A river, iron-grey in the winter light, meandered through the peaceful French countryside.

Biggles flew low, alert for anything out of the ordinary. But everything appeared quite normal. Baffled, he was about to nudge the rudder-bar to bring the Strutter round on a reciprocal course when something – an almost imperceptible movement – caught his eye.

He stiffened, bared his teeth in a triumphant grin, and yelled over his shoulder, 'That's it! Hold on!'

Hardly had Jim heard him when the aircraft banked steeply to port, engine howling, throwing Jim hard against the side of the cockpit. Shaken, bruised, frozen and half-deafened, the young American hung on grimly, telling himself that this mysterious *it* had better be worth what he was enduring.

4

THE SECRET WEAPON

The fields and hedgerows rushed towards them in a green blur as Biggles took the Sopwith Strutter as low as he dared, which, as far as Jim was concerned, seemed verging on the suicidal. But then, he knew nothing of Biggles' remarkable skill and finesse as a pilot; of the young airman's almost legendary reputation throughout all the squadrons of the Royal Flying Corps.

Had he known, Jim might have felt more at ease; though whether his stomach would have appreciated the distinction is doubtful.

Biggles was pointing ahead of them and slightly to the right, and Jim's eyes ached as he searched for something out of the ordinary in what seemed to be pleasant, rolling countryside. It looked perfectly normal – certainly nothing to have caused Biggles' obvious jubilation and excitement. Then, to his surprise, rather like a magical conjuring trick suddenly revealed to him, Jim *did* see something – as if part of a green hillside had moved. It wasn't a green hillside at all, Jim saw, peering through the windscreen, but a huge area of camouflage netting, the size of a football field, with something moving underneath it.

A large circular object, as near as he could tell, on the end of a long, jointed metal arm. Jim had no idea what it was. In some ways it reminded him of a radar dish, or radio-telescope antenna, neither of which had been invented in World War I.

The whole apparatus was rising up, the concave dish turning towards them like a single malevolent eye, as Biggles lined up the machine with a feather-light touch to right rudder, and pressed the black rubber bulb in rapid succession. The camera shutter clicked four times.

As the camouflaged installation flashed by under their starboard wingtip, Biggles hauled back on the stick and practically stood the Strutter on its tail. The engine howled on all nine cylinders as the wooden prop kicked the air behind them and clawed the machine vertically into the sky.

Jim swallowed his breakfast for the second time that day and hung on for grim death.

'Better brace yourself!' Biggles shouted to him above the engine's fearful racket and the icy blasting slipstream. 'It's starting again – the vibration!'

What now? Jim wondered, not sure how much more he could take.

His first intimation that something strange was happening was when a shudder ran through the air-craft, rattling every nut, bolt and spar, including the fillings in Jim's teeth. The vibration steadily increased in pitch and intensity, and with it came a shrill humming that seemed to drive needles of ultrasonic sound through Jim's brain. At any moment, he felt, they would be shaken into a thousand tiny bits and pieces.

'What's wrong with the plane?' he yelled through cupped hands.

'It's not just the plane,' Biggles shouted back, and jerked his thumb at the wings. 'Look!'

The wings were glowing with an eerie orange light. Along each strut and cross-braced wire there danced a shimmering nimbus of bright orange, like St Elmo's fire.

Grim-faced, Biggles stared at the wings, shaking his head. 'Exactly the same as before,' he told Jim stonily. 'But this time I'll try a little less altitude . . .'

And with that he pushed the joystick forward with both hands and kicked at the rudder bar. The nose dipped and the Strutter hurtled earthwards in a screaming power dive.

Jim clamped his hands to his ears as the high-pitched humming shrilled painfully through his head. The entire aircraft was bathed in the orange glow, vibrating madly and threatening at any moment to break up. Neither men nor machine could take much more, that was clear.

Jarred loose by the vibration and speed of descent, the large box-shaped camera broke free of its mounting and dangled beneath the lower wing on the end of the remote-control cable. But Biggles had other problems on his mind. Knuckles white with the strain, mouth set in a thin straight line, he fought to bring the aircraft out of its steep dive. Using all his strength, he wrenched the joystick into the pit of his stomach and levelled out above the green fields, flipping one wing to avoid a grove of trees.

There were cold beads of perspiration on Biggles'

furrowed brow. He wiped them away with the back of his gloved hand. That was a damn close call.

Jim took his hands away from his ears. The humming had ceased and the aircraft was no longer vibrating. He looked at the wings and saw that the orange glow had also faded. He sagged with relief, but then quickly sat up, eyes widening with alarm as he noticed that the camera was gone from its mounting.

He leaned forward and urgently tapped Biggles on the shoulder, pointing downwards.

Biggles nodded sternly. 'Take over!' he rapped out, and to Jim's horror released his straps and swung one leg over the side of the cockpit.

Jim's stomach turned to water. 'Take over what?'

This guy couldn't be serious – but he was, Jim saw, staring with stricken eyes as Biggles clambered out on to the wing.

'You're crazy!' Jim yelled at him. 'I'll kill us both!'

He looked down inside the cockpit, and out of a sense of sheer self-preservation grabbed the stick and planted both feet on the rudder bar. At once the aircraft yawed sickeningly, causing Biggles to hang on to one of the wooden support struts.

'Hold her steady!'

The next few minutes lasted an eternity for Jim as he watched the young pilot, spreadeagled on the wing, reach down over the leading edge and pull the camera up by its cable. With one arm hooked around a strut, he got a grip on the square box, flipped open the hinged back and removed the wooden-framed film plate.

'I've got the film – here, take it!' Biggles cried, holding it out at full stretch.

Jim took the plate and stowed it beside him. Meanwhile Biggles was struggling to release the heavy box camera, which finally dropped away from the cable.

At that precise moment the Strutter decided, for reasons of its own, to go into a spin. Used to driving a car, and not knowing what else to do, Jim looked stupidly for the brake. The engine note rose to a shrill tormented whine as the aircraft spun out of control, dropping like a stone, the green earth whirling dizzily round and round Jim's head.

As if in slow-motion, resisting the fierce centrifugal pressure that threatened to fling him out into space, Biggles hauled himself hand over painful hand across the wing until he was able to get a grip on the edge of the cockpit. With a final mighty heave that took every ounce of his strength, he tumbled inside and fought to stabilise the controls. Although a sluggish machine generally, the Strutter was inherently stable, with two air-brake flaps in the lower wings, and gradually it responded to Biggles' expert touch.

Moments later they were back on an even keel, the horizon back in its rightful place, and flying serenely in the direction of the dull reddish globe of the setting sun.

The operational airfield of No. 266 Squadron, RFC, comprised a jumble of hastily erected wooden buildings which served as hangars, tents for the ground crews, and the broken-down, smoke-blackened walls of what had been a French farm-house. A rather bedraggled windsock blew stiffly on top of a pole next to the dispersal point. Biggles side-slipped gently and floated the Strutter down over the grass strip to a faultless dead-stick landing.

As the machine rolled to a halt he jumped to the ground, discarding his flying-kit, and beamed up at Jim, two white circles outlining his eyes against his dirt and oil-begrimed face.

'We were damn lucky!' announced Biggles cheerfully. 'Got the plates?'

Jim gave a weak grin and held the photographic plates aloft.

With a trembling hand he tugged off his goggles, his face white as a sheet under the grime, and stood up in the cockpit on rubbery legs.

'Don't drop 'em!' called out Biggles anxiously, as Jim swayed to and fro.

' – I'm gonna be sick.'

'Go ahead – it's nothing to be ashamed of,' answered Biggles, a twinkle of amusement in his eyes.

Jim suddenly slapped his hand over his mouth. He stared cross-eyed at his fingers, which were surrounded by a pale yellow glow. The glow quickly spread to his hand and down his arm. With a low groan Jim clutched feebly at the side of the cockpit. His legs flew up in the air as he toppled backwards out of sight.

In alarm, Biggles leapt over the tail-plane and ran round to the opposite side of the machine. There he pulled up short, an expression of blank incredulity creeping over his face.

'Hey! Where are you?' he called out sharply, ducking down to look underneath the fuselage. He straightened up and peered inside the empty cockpit, totally perplexed.

Biggles stepped back and gazed all around, scratching his head in consternation. 'And where are my bloody film plates?' he muttered through clenched teeth.

* * *

Seeing Jim disappear with a despairing lunge behind Arnold Schwarzenegger's oiled torso, Debbie pushed and jostled her way through the crowd to reach him. Before she got there she heard the sound of somebody being violently ill. The placard shook as the horrible retching continued, and Jim backed out, wiping his mouth with his sleeve, holding something close to his chest.

The silence in the banqueting suite had the quality of mass hypnosis. Eyes bulged and mouths hung open at the instantaneous transformation that had taken place.

Jim's hair looked like it had been in a whirlwind. His face was blackened with dirt and smeared with oil. His white dinner-jacket, immaculate only moments before, was now crumpled, grimy and oil-spattered, with the left sleeve practically torn away in a great ragged gash.

And Jim himself had been transformed into a dazed and wild-eyed paranoid wreck, backing away from the astonished stares of the stunned and silent crowd.

'Jim!' Debbie cried, darting forward and grabbing his arm. 'What is it, what's wrong? Shall I get a doctor?'

Jim's throat worked. He shook his head dumbly.

'I told him the corn was made out of dog puke,' Maxine Fine informed a goggling Chuck, standing beside her.

Clutching the photographic plates to his chest, Jim turned and stumbled towards the door. Debbie ran after him.

'Jim, wait!'

'Just – leave me alone.'

'What's wrong?' Tears sprang to Debbie's eyes. 'Jim, please tell me!'

Jim leaned against a pillar, chest heaving, his distraught and blackened face misted with sweat.

'I – I can't explain it . . .'

Debbie reached out and touched his shoulder. Her hand recoiled as the sleeve fell open, slashed right through to his bare arm.

'What happened to your sleeve?'

'They must have shot me,' Jim murmured, blinking slowly.

'Shot you?' Debbie gaped at him. 'Jim, what's *happening*?'

Jim pushed her aside and staggered towards the door.

'Where are you going?'

'London,' Jim said, and was gone, leaving a helpless and tearful Debbie gazing after him.

5

RIDDLES AND ANSWERS

It was a raw, dismal day, a cold wind snapping at the gold-tasselled flag on the white turret of the Tower of London as the black cab turned left past the Royal Mint and entered the northern approach to Tower Bridge. The two great square turreted edifices of pale stone, with their narrow slits of leaded glass, stood firmly planted on either bank of the Thames, like stern and rather forbidding guardians of the old dockland area. They had witnessed the clippers and the iron-sided steamships, the dreadnoughts and destroyers, and now presided over a small armada of yachts, canal narrowboats and floating homes in St Katherine's Dock.

'This is Tower Bridge, mate,' the cabbie advised Jim, swinging into the kerbside. 'You'll have to find 1–A yourself.'

Jim paid the fare and hopped out on to the cold pavement, tugging the collar of his windcheater around his ears, and looked about him. Two solid streams of traffic poured across the narrow roadway. A few tugs, barges and other small craft chugged up and down the broad grey river. There was nothing large in sight for the moment, requiring the raising of the two connecting spans.

Odd sort of place to live, Jim thought, feeling a twinge of unease and doubt. He hoped his three thousand mile trip was going to be worth the time and trouble, not to mention the nervous strain. But he was determined to get to the bottom of this.

Jim spotted the address, No. 1–A, almost at once.

It was engraved in the stone lintel above a heavy timber door reinforced with iron rivets which was embedded deeply in the base of one of the towers. Not finding a bellpush, Jim knocked, the echoes dying away emptily, and when no one answered, turned the wrought iron ring which served as a handle and entered. He found himself in a dim, shadowy room filled with heavy machinery; the dense smell of engine oil and musty river damp mingled in the air, catching the back of his throat. Jim nodded to himself as he realised that the huge winches, blocks and thick steel cables must be the mechanism for raising the bridge. There was no one about, so he guessed that it was remotely operated from somewhere by the bridge-master.

Behind the drums and cables and electrical switch-gear Jim came upon a metal stairway rising steeply into the darkness of the high-ceilinged room. Gripping the rail, he climbed slowly and cautiously, his eyes gradually becoming accustomed to the gloom. The stairway ended in a wooden door, almost medieval in character, bound in iron strips and rising to a curved point at the top.

Jim steadied his breathing and raised his fist. Before his knuckles could make contact, however, the door swung eerily and silently open. Jim froze, and then took a tentative step forward and peered inside curiously.

His first impression was that he had wandered by mistake into a museum of some kind.

Shifting patterns of firelight reflected on the panelled walls and ornate plaster ceiling. In the deeper recesses, shelves of leather-bound books with gold-embossed spines gave off rich burnished gleams. A stained-glass window made a mosaic of colour on the thick carpet, also throwing into prominence a large gilt-framed portrait of Queen Victoria. And everywhere Jim looked there were items of military memorabilia and racks of antiquated weaponry, every wall covered with framed photographs, documents, maps, rolls of honour and ribboned medals under glass.

On a polished brass perch next to a narrow leaded window overlooking the river, a black raven with a yellow beak regarded him with a haughty, disapproving eye.

The trim, spare figure with thinning grey hair seated in the winged armchair facing away from Jim hadn't moved once.

'I've been expecting you,' said Colonel Raymond in his quiet, courtly voice, without glancing up from the book he was reading. 'Do come in, Mr Ferguson.'

He now closed the book, after marking the place, and turned his head. A faint smile of gentle amusement played over his fine-boned, ascetic features.

'This is my lair – as I call it. Rather cosy. Of course when they raise the bridge it gets a bit noisy. But that's not too often.' He extended a thin, gracious hand. 'Please come and sit down. I'll make some tea.'

'Forget the tea,' said Jim rudely, ignoring the chair Colonel Raymond had indicated. 'Would you mind telling me what you're up to? I have a business to run – people relying on me.' He pointed his finger and went on angrily, 'I don't know what you're doing or why, but stop it – do you hear me, stop it!'

'Mr Ferguson, please don't shout.'

Jim spread his arms. 'Why did you stick *me* with this?' he pleaded hoarsely.

'If I had to "stick" someone with this – as you so eloquently put it – I would not have picked you,' Colonel Raymond told him gravely. 'Fighting for your country and your life is something, thankfully, you have never had to do.'

'That's just where you're wrong.' Jim uttered a short cynical bark of a laugh. 'On the last escapade I was on, I was shot at by some black-hooded clown in a black airplane!'

Raymond pressed a fingertip to his lips and glanced away. 'Von Stalhein – had to be!' He looked up at Jim, the faded blue eyes taking on a harder glint. 'Please sit down, Mr Ferguson. I'll tell you what I know.'

Feeling he was getting somewhere at last, Jim unfastened his coat and took the chair opposite Raymond.

The colonel regarded him pensively for a moment. Then he said quietly, 'The man you met was James Bigglesworth.' From a table nearby he took a photograph in a silver frame and handed it to Jim. 'This is Biggles with his team. Algy, Bertie and Ginger.'

That was the guy he had met, all right, Jim saw, studying the photograph, got up in his World War I flying gear. No mistaking that keen, thoughtful face and determined jaw. Algy was tall and lanky with the casual air of an aristocrat, Bertie shorter, rounder, with a moustache and monocle, while Ginger appeared to be the youngest, a grinning freckle-faced character with a look of cheerful optimism.

Jim returned the photograph to Colonel Raymond.

'Algy, Bertie and Ginger. With Biggles. Sounds like a vaudeville act.'

'Indeed not,' Colonel Raymond reproved him gently, glancing once more at the group before putting the photograph back, his eyes misty and faraway. 'They were four of the bravest men it has been my privilege to know. A lot of the freedom we now all take for granted we owe to men like them.'

'What has this got to do with me?' asked Jim patiently.

'You gave this to Biggles.' Colonel Raymond took a card carefully wrapped in clear plastic from his pocket.

Jim recognised it straight away. 'How the hell did you get that?'

'Biggles gave it to me.'

'When?'

'Almost seventy years ago,' reflected Colonel Raymond sadly. 'You see, I was his commanding officer on the Western Front.'

Jim took the card and turned it over wonderingly in his fingers. It was crumpled at the edges and yellow with age, the print faded and cracked. It read: Jim Ferguson. Celebrity Dinners.

He glanced up sharply at Colonel Raymond. 'I just gave him this card two nights ago. Are you saying that was in 1917?'

'Time travel is not unknown in history,' Raymond said, holding out his hand for the card and tucking it away. He raised an eyebrow. 'There is evidence that it happens more often than anyone suspects . . .'

'But why me ?'

'I don't know the *why* of it,' replied the colonel with a slight shrug. 'Only that it happens.'

Jim brushed his hand through his hair. 'But why do I keep meeting Biggles?' he persisted.

'Well, as to that,' said Colonel Raymond mildly, yet with total seriousness, 'I think Biggles is your time twin.'

'Time twin?' Jim cried, not sure whether or not he was expected to laugh. 'You got anything stronger than tea?'

Colonel Raymond spread his hands. 'It seems for the moment that your lives are inextricably interwoven. I wish I could explain it, Mr Ferguson. The reasons are unknown, and perhaps, unknowable.'

Jim rummaged in the large inner pocket of his coat and withdrew the photographic plate. He held it up. 'Could the reason have something to do with this?'

Raymond's whole manner changed. Taking the plate from Jim, he examined it with intense curiosity, his long thin hands trembling slightly. 'An old aerial photographic plate. How did you get hold of it?'

'When I went back the second time, Biggles and I were on a photographic mission.' Jim gave a rueful grin and inclined his head. 'I was holding that thing when I returned.'

Colonel Raymond was now staring at Jim. He moistened his lips and leaned forward in his chair, the shifting firelight emphasising the long hollows of his cheeks.

'Did Biggles tell you what these photographs are?'

Jim nodded. 'Yeah, some kind of secret weapon. Biggles seemed real concerned about it – he said something about a big enemy attack coming up in two days, and unless the weapon was destroyed the Germans intended using it.'

Raymond got up with surprising agility and began pacing, the plate clasped in his hands. He swung round, as if suddenly coming to a decision, his eyes glittering with barely suppressed excitement and resolve.

'It's time for action, Mr Ferguson,' he announced firmly.

'What kind of action?' asked Jim warily.

But already the colonel was striding across the room to a tall cupboard next to the stained-glass window. 'First I'll get these photographs processed. Second, we must get you prepared,' he went on, opening the cupboard door and lifting out a large, heavy bag of well-worn leather, the corners reinforced with brass.

'Prepared?' Jim said, rising slowly to his feet.

'For your next trip.' Colonel Raymond brought the leather bag across and dumped it at Jim's feet. Something metallic clinked inside. 'This time we'll send you to the battlefield with the proper kit.'

Jim didn't like the sound of this. In fact he positively hated it. The mere thought of returning to the past – and *that* past in particular – gave him a sinking, queasy feeling in the pit of his stomach.

He said bleakly, 'Isn't there any way I can get out of it?'

'I'm afraid not. Ever read the stories of King Arthur and Merlin?'

'Sure.'

'Merlin was a time-traveller, like you. He was compelled to help King Arthur in times of trouble – just as you seem to be helping Biggles.'

Jim nodded glumly. Not much of a consolation, he was thinking.

'How long will I keep going back?'

'Until you set history right again.' Colonel Raymond paused, looking grave. 'Or until you and Biggles are killed.'

Jim gulped and stared down at the bag. After a momentary hesitation he picked it up. He staggered a little under its weight as Raymond walked him to the door.

'If the enemy *has* developed a secret weapon that allows them to break through the allied lines,' Raymond explained, 'the Germans may well win the First World War. History would be altered. You would be stuck in 1917, a sort of time-orphan, I suppose.' He sighed gloomily. 'And God knows what would happen to the rest of us.'

'Jesus!' Jim exclaimed. The raven was watching him with its beady, supercilious eye.

'You must not fail.'

The weight of his words hung more heavily on Jim than the leather bag dragging at his arm.

'Well!' Colonel Raymond brightened and clapped

him on the shoulder. 'I think you're ready. I've made arrangements for you to stay in the Tower Hotel, not far from here across the river. I'll contact you when the plates have been developed.' He shook Jim's hand warmly. 'Good luck!'

Jim hoisted the bag across his shoulder as Raymond opened the door and stood aside. Jim summoned up his bravest, most confident smile, which didn't come out the way he intended, and to Colonel Raymond's keen eye wasn't entirely convincing.

'You're in good hands,' he said stoutly, and went on to reassure the young American: 'Biggles was a fine officer.'

Jim didn't doubt it for an instant. But Biggles or no Biggles, he had serious doubts about the part he, Jim Ferguson of Celebrity Dinners, New York, NY, was supposed to play in keeping history on the right track. Why me? he thought as he started down the iron stairway. *Why me?*

6

GOOD NEWS, BAD NEWS

'Did you see these orders?' Bill's bearded face split in a wide grin as he slapped a thick sheaf of carbon flimsies on Debbie's desk. He stood there beaming, hands on hips. 'Nearly every chain in the country wants us. Even one from Maxine Fine – one hundred thousand pieces!'

Debbie cradled the phone against her cheek. Her eyes looked dark from worry and lack of sleep, her smooth pale complexion in startling contrast to her glowing auburn hair, swept back from her face. She smiled wanly.

'I saw them. It's great,' she said listlessly. She perked up, paying close attention to the voice on the phone, and said, 'Yes, okay. Thank you. I'll hold.'

Bill propped himself on the edge of the desk and gazed pensively down at her. 'I guess all these orders don't mean much without Jim, do they?'

'Is it so obvious?' said Debbie, putting on a brave smile.

Bill leaned nearer. 'I'll tell you a secret. He feels the same way about you.'

'Bill, what made him act like that?' Debbie asked worriedly. 'He was never – '

The door crashed open to admit Chuck. In his chubby paw he carried a ponderous tome, several inches thick and weighing at least a couple of pounds. His face was wreathed in several smiles.

'Psychosis Trauma,' he pronounced grandly, tapping the book's cover. 'Say's so right here.'

Bill bent his head to read the title. '*Diseases of the Mind*.' He looked at Debbie and closed his eyes painfully.

But as usual, Chuck was unstoppable. When he had an idea fixed in his mind nitro-glycerine wouldn't shake it loose.

'I've been reading all night and I found the answer.' Chuck inserted a fat thumb, flipped open a page, and pointed at an entry. 'Psychosis Trauma Syndrome! Guys like Jim – pushy over-achievers – they store up stress, see, and it builds up inside until they just *snap*!'

He slammed the book shut. Startled, Bill opened his eyes and looked glassily at the wall, shaking his head.

'Now here's the good news,' Chuck told them, in full flow now. 'The way they bring these weirdos back to normal is with *shock*. We gotta find Jim and confront him – ' Chuck swelled up for the big finish ' – with *something shocking*!'

Bill groaned out loud. 'That's supposed to be *electric shock*, you nerd,' he said scathingly.

'Yeah, well,' Chuck shrugged. 'That works good too.'

'Jim's not crazy. He's scared,' Debbie put in loyally. 'It's got something to do with that man who came to see him. I'm afraid it's some kind of blackmail – '

She broke off and spoke into the phone, her voice rising with excitement. 'Hello?' She glanced up at the two men, her face suddenly transformed, radiant with happiness. 'It's Jim!' She said anxiously into the phone, 'Where are you?'

'I'm at the Tower Hotel, London.' Even over the three thousand mile transatlantic cable Debbie could detect the slight strain in Jim's voice. 'How are the orders coming?' he asked her, making an effort to seem casual and relaxed.

'We're in business. Jim, we've cracked it.'

'I'll be home in a few days.'

'What's going on?' asked Debbie with a frown, curious and concerned in equal measure.

'It's personal. I can handle it.' Jim's reply was clipped, almost brusque, reviving Debbie's fears all over again.

'I can be on the next plane – '

'No! Absolutely not! You stay there. I'll be back soon. I promise.'

'Okay, Jim.' Debbie glanced up at Bill and Chuck. 'We all love you.' She lowered her eyes and whispered into the phone, 'Especially me.'

'I love you too.'

Debbie replaced the receiver with a puzzled, rather wistful smile. She stared at it for a second or two, her hazel eyes hardening. She looked up with a determined tilt to her jaw.

'I'm going to London.'

'I'm going with you,' said Bill promptly, straightening up.

'Me too!' said Chuck eagerly, not to be left out.

'Wait, Bill.' Debbie got swiftly to her feet, raising two slender palms. 'Somebody's got to stay here and handle the orders.'

'You can't go over there alone!' Bill objected.

'I'll take Chuck.'

Bill opened his mouth to protest, then thought better of it when he saw the hard glint of steel in Debbie's eyes. He gave a weary shrug of defeat.

Chuck was delighted. His face wore a fat, triumphant smirk as he brandished the heavy medical book. 'Jim is as good as cured,' he declared smugly.

* * *

'More local thunderstorms are predicted for the London area, continuing throughout the night, decreasing by morning. Motorists are warned of high winds and possible flooding . . .'

You're not kidding, Jim thought, wincing a little as a roll of thunder drowned out the rest of the TV weatherman's forecast. He looked towards the balcony window, noting with anxious eyes the storm-clouds tumbling in over the river, dark and bruised and angry. He was in for a rough night – perhaps in more senses than one.

Colonel Raymond had certainly been true to his word in 'preparing' Jim for whatever ordeal lay ahead – even down to the period detail.

He must make an incongruous sight, Jim reflected, sitting here in his perfectly ordinary 1980s hotel room, with its double bed, wall closet, pale blue fitted carpet and TV babbling away to itself in the corner – dressed and kitted out as a 'Tommy' from World War I.

For the past hour he had been waiting with some trepidation and discomfort in steel helmet, khaki tunic, tight leggings, and stout lace-up boots, ammunition bandoliers slung over one shoulder and box-type gas mask across the other, a heavy sub-machine-gun cradled in his lap. Several times, as the lightning flickered over the wet slate rooftops, Jim had tensed and glanced down at his hands, half-expecting to see the tell-tale blue sparks arcing between his fingertips. So far, however, his fearful expectations hadn't been realised. Nothing had happened – except for cramp in his calves and chafing around his forehead where the helmet fitted a pinch too snugly.

Jim gritted his teeth, hands gripping the weapon tightly, at another flash of lightning and rolling peal of thunder.

Slowly he raised and inspected his trembling hand, and then sagged back in the chair, a surge of relief flooding through him. He closed his eyes and yawned. All at once he felt very tired.

Settling himself as comfortably as he was able in the constraining ill-fitting gear, Jim breathed deeply and drifted into shallow troubled sleep.

The Germans had activated the secret weapon. Its insistent droning hum was everywhere, getting louder . . . and louder . . . and louder . . .

There was no escape. Jim tried to run but the stiff uniform and cumbersome equipment were hindering him. As the humming swelled to a screech, Jim's eyes snapped open in the broad daylight of his hotel room. He goggled. A middle-aged woman in a cleaner's smock was backing towards him, oblivious of his presence as she busily wheeled a droning vacuum cleaner to and fro across the carpet.

Jim looked down at himself, then reacting swiftly, slid the machine-gun out of sight underneath his chair. The woman sensed the movement and turned, her jaw falling slackly open at finding a young man kitted out for battle in room 1231 of the Tower Hotel.

Seeing the panic in her eyes, Jim got stiffly to his feet, and gave a weak, self-conscious grin. He tapped the steel helmet, feeling foolish and thinking fast.

'Ah . . . I was at a masquerade party,' he explained lamely.

'Excuse me, sir,' mumbled the woman, edging towards the door, now seeing the funny side of things. 'I didn't see you there. I'll come back later.'

She covered her mouth, and with shoulders shaking ran from the room, dragging the vacuum behind her.

Jim stood at the window, looking out over the peaceful skyline of a bright London morning. Far below, the wide sweep of the Thames sparkled in the sunshine. Traffic buzzed in the streets, red double-decker buses and black beetle cabs negotiating the sharp bend on Tower Hill. One of those cabs, turning left into Byward Street in front of the hotel, had but Jim known it, contained a pretty young woman with auburn hair and a perspiring whale of a man in a check overcoat and pork pie hat – who not two hours before had landed at Heathrow Airport.

Yawning, Jim pulled off the helmet, and flexed his aching shoulders. He rubbed his chin, feeling in desperate need of a shave, shower, and a large breakfast of eggs and bacon washed down with strong black coffee.

Moments later he had discarded the khaki uniform and all its trappings and was standing naked in front of the bathroom mirror, running his battery-powered electric shaver over his bristly chin.

So the colonel's prediction hadn't come true after all, Jim mused happily. The elaborate preparation and long hours of tense waiting had all been for nothing. Maybe, he fervently hoped, he wasn't going to be flung violently into the past ever again. With a bit of luck that particular past was, quite literally, behind him for good.

His buoyant mood was spoiled somewhat when his razor suddenly developed a glitch. The damn thing kept cutting out on him. Jim sighed with irritation and shook it, and as he did so the colour drained from his face. Thousands of tiny blue flashing sparks were dancing over the plastic casing. Like a runaway electrical storm they spread down his bare arm, on to his shoulder and across his chest, until his entire body was enveloped in bright flaring arcs of plasma.

Jim staggered back from the mirror, grabbed a towel and whipped it round his middle. Still clutching the razor, he made a desperate lunge for the bedroom. But as he charged through the bathroom door, the bedroom ceased to exist.

His naked foot met no resistance and he felt himself to be falling . . . falling . . . endlessly falling into a black pit of nothingness.

* * *

The sisters of mercy had been about to partake of a simple meal when the apparition materialised from nowhere before them.

Seated at the long wooden table in the convent refectory, a large plain room with beamed ceiling and a carved oak crucifix displayed on the whitewashed wall, they were bowing their heads over steaming bowls of soup and listening to the gentle dignified voice of the Mother Superior intoning grace when it happened.

A handsome, broad-shouldered young man, naked except for a towel, appeared out of thin air and crashed down on to the table, scattering bowls and dishes in all directions. As he lay there, dazed, spreadeagled amidst the wreckage, the focus of ten pairs of startled eyes, not a soul dared move. Then a young nun, pale to the lips, quickly crossed herself. Another nearly fainted and had to grab the table for support. The Mother Superior covered her face with both hands before peeking through her fingers.

Yes, the apparition was still there. Had they been chosen, the Blessed Order of St Teresa, to be witnesses to a miracle?

Jim shook his head to clear it and sat up. In his left hand he held the buzzing shaver. He switched it off and looked round at the nuns in their plain grey habits, gazing at him in stricken silence. On their heads they wore huge white winged bonnets, partially concealing their round eyes and shocked faces.

The young nun who had hurriedly crossed herself leaned over the table towards him. '*Etes-vous Jesus Christ?*' she asked in a breathless whisper.

'Biggles! Where is he?' Jim searched each face for an answer. But all he received were blank, uncomprehending stares. His voice sharpened, became urgent, imperative.

'Bigglesworth! Captain James Bigglesworth! He's got to be here!'

Rather late in the day it struck Jim that he was practically naked in a roomful of nuns. The Mother Superior's expression of surprise and dumbstruck awe had changed to one of suspicion bordering on hostility. Jim tucked the towel between his legs and slid off the table, backing away across the tiled floor.

'Biggles?' he tried again, clearing his throat. 'Does that ring a bell?'

In unison the nuns turned their white winged bonnets to watch him. Jim retreated further under their scrutiny and unnerving silence.

A silence in the long bare room that was suddenly shattered by the hollow, echoing tramp of marching boots. Before Jim could even turn at the sound he was seized roughly by the elbows and propelled forward, spun round, and thrust against the whitewashed wall. Three grim-faced men in an assortment of leather flying gear and battledress stood in a tight semi-circle round him. They each carried a large and very efficient-looking service revolver, held in a manner that suggested they knew how to use them.

'*Qui êtes-vous*?' demanded one of them harshly, fixing Jim with a gimlet eye through a gleaming monocle. '*Etes-vous Belge*?'

Jim blinked rapidly, trying to take in this new turn of events. 'Not Belge,' he protested, shaking his head. He tapped his bare chest. 'I'm Jim Ferguson.'

'You're an American,' said the one with the monocle and small military moustache in a tone of quiet wonder.

'That's right.' Jim's eyes narrowed a fraction. He

began to smile. 'You're Bertie, right?' Jim's smile widened as he saw the three of them exchange startled looks.

He pointed to the lanky one in the officer's hat. 'Algy.'

And to the youngest of them. 'Ginger.'

Jim folded his arms. 'Not so good on faces, but monocles I never forget!' he told them cheerfully.

'How did you get here?' drawled Algy suspiciously, who on the official rolls of the RFC was known somewhat grandly as Flight-Lieutenant the Honourable Algernon Montgomery Lacey. He much preferred Algy.

'You wouldn't believe it,' Jim sighed.

'Try us,' suggested Bertie softly, raising his revolver and pointing it at Jim's heart.

Jim shrugged weakly. 'I fell through a hole in time.'

There was a momentary dead silence. Then Algy smiled coldly and said casually, 'Oh, you can do better than that.'

'It's the truth,' Jim asserted, though he didn't hold out much hope of being believed; his voice sounded unconvincing even in his own ears.

Bertie cocked the hammer on his revolver. 'You have three seconds.' Despite his rather comical appearance, and his reputation as something of a wag, always ready with a wry quip or sardonic remark, Bertie Lissie was nobody's fool. His finger tightened on the trigger. 'One . . . two . . .'

'Okay.' Jim held up both hands. 'I'm an American secret agent,' he lied glibly.

'Where's your identification?' asked Ginger at once.

'Oh, come on, you don't want to see it,' said Jim helplessly, gesturing at his own nakedness. 'Look, you know we don't carry identification!'

'Why are you wearing that towel?' Bertie put in curiously.

'Because I was taking a bath,' retorted Jim wearily.

This reply wasn't appreciated, or found to be in the least amusing. Jim could see that right away as Algy pressed the muzzle of the revolver to Jim's temple.

'Try again,' he suggested softly.

Jim had run out of answers. By the look of things he had run out of time too. He glanced past Bertie's shoulder as a shadowy figure loomed in the doorway, and then came into the room with a brisk, confident step.

'Release him,' ordered Biggles, striding forward, a genial smile playing about his lips. 'He once saved my life. That's good enough for me.' He moved into the circle and stood with hands on hips, surveying Jim's predicament with a twinkle of amusement.

'Glad to have you on board.'

His three comrades-in-arms regarded Jim with new interest.

'Is this the chap who stowed away on your aeroplane?' Ginger Hebblethwaite inquired of his chief, eyebrows raised in astonishment.

'The same.' Biggles shot a shrewd glance at Jim. 'What did you do with my photo plates?' he asked bluntly.

'They're being developed. In the meantime my orders are to help you guys anyway I can.' Jim shivered and wrapped his arms across his chest. 'Can I get some clothes? It's freezing in here!'

Biggles took care of the matter straight away. After a quiet word with the Mother Superior some garments were produced and Jim was handed a long, grey shift in coarse woollen material. There were some stifled giggles amongst the sisters as Jim held the garment up against himself, and discovered it to be a nun's habit.

'My favourite colour,' he quipped, trying not to blush.

Bertie grinned and nudged Algy in the ribs. Ginger hid a smirk. But there was little time for frivolity, as Biggles' stern expression made plain.

'Put it on quickly,' he commanded crisply. His jaw tightened as he went on, 'We've got work to do.'

7

BETRAYED?

The tall, dignified figure of the Mother Superior glided smoothly along the chill and rather gloomy stone corridors of the convent, her sandalled feet making no sound on the flagged floor. Following behind her long rustling skirts, Jim strode along with Biggles, sensing in the general mood of the party a heightened pitch of tension. Even Bertie had fallen silent. Algy was his usual taciturn self, while Ginger's youthful face was set in a pugnacious frown, reminding Jim of a scowling cherub.

There could be no doubt that some pretty grim business lay ahead of them. Jim's uneasy curiosity was aroused.

In response to his query, Biggles gestured to the bleak, flat, almost treeless countryside glimpsed through the narrow glassless windows, covered in a thin scattering of snow. The sky was pale and cloudless, a watery sun casting weak shadows.

Beyond the convent wall, Jim caught sight of a white marble statue of Madonna and Child, raised high on a granite plinth.

'We're ten miles behind enemy lines,' explained

Biggles in a low voice. 'We're here to meet someone who has information on the German secret weapon.'

Before Jim could press him further, the Mother Superior paused outside a pair of double-doors. She turned, and, with one hand on the latch, touched a finger to her lips, indicating silence.

Biggles nodded curtly and glanced over his shoulder. 'Bertie, Algy – go and check the perimeter.'

As they moved off down the corridor, unbuckling the flaps on their leather holsters, Biggles turned back to the Mother Superior, who was holding the door open for them to enter.

Silently they filed inside. The hushed atmosphere was that of a chapel – which it had been – and also of a hospital ward, which it was now. Beneath the high vaulted ceiling, supported by thick stone columns, and under the pitying plaster gaze of the Madonna from her white marble pedestal in the nave, row upon row of the injured and the dying lay on stretchers and trestle beds, taking up virtually every inch of space, tended by the sisters of mercy in their white starched bonnets and aprons. Several of the pews had been pushed into a corner to form an operating area. The little entrance hall leading from the main door had been turned into a temporary mortuary. Over everything hung the sweetish sickly smell of chloroform and the stench of open wounds.

A hard, flat light came into Biggles' eyes as he took in the scene, noting with a cold fury that these were not combat troops, but ordinary civilians – innocent and defenceless men, women and children trampled and crushed under the enemy's iron heel.

Biggles started slightly as the Mother Superior touched his arm. With an effort he controlled his simmering anger. She was pointing to a young girl to the shadowy rear of the chapel who was bending over a stretcher, holding a cup for an old man with a bloodstained bandage round his head. Biggles nodded, signalling to Jim and Ginger to remain where they were, and was about to follow the Mother Superior through the closely packed beds when the girl turned her head, a curtain of dark hair falling across her eyes.

From a few feet away, Jim saw the colour visibly drain from Biggles' taut face. The airman stared as if he'd seen a ghost. A muscle twitched in his cheek.

By Jim's side, Ginger too reacted in a startled fashion. His fair eyebrows sprang up like faint brushmarks over his wide blue eyes. 'Marie!' Jim heard him say in a shocked whisper.

Jim watched Biggles thread his way to the girl, and muttered out of the corner of his mouth, 'Who's Marie?'

Ginger rubbed the side of his face. 'A girl that Biggles met in 1916 – seems she was a German agent who tried to trick Biggles into carrying messages over the lines.' He shook his head and gave a rueful smile. 'She fell in love with him though, and double-crossed her own side to save his neck. Now both sides want her for the firing squad.'

He registered the concern in Jim's face, and added confidentially, 'Don't worry, Biggles won't be taken in twice.'

Marie straightened up slowly at Biggles' approach.

Her dark liquid eyes mirrored her inner confusion, tinged with some alarm. Clearly, she had not expected this.

'You know each other?' inquired the Mother Superior alertly, looking from one to the other with an air of mild surprise.

'Yes,' averred Biggles, his eyes locked on Marie's. 'We have met.'

There followed a charged, tense moment of silence, and then, moistening her lips, Marie said in an urgent, husky voice, 'I have the information you need. But first look . . .'

Her small, neat figure swung round and she gestured with a pale hand to where two nuns were drawing a white sheet over the bodies of a man and a woman. Biggles had time for only a brief glimpse, but it was enough. His dark brows came together, his lips curling in horrified disgust.

'Their bodies were turned to jelly,' Marie informed him in a low, trembling tone. 'They must have suffered an agonising death.'

Biggles glanced round stonily. Time was running out and this was a dangerous place to be.

'Where can we talk alone?' he asked the girl.

Without a word, the Mother Superior bowed slightly and moved discreetly away. Biggles followed Marie to the transept adjoining the nave and down three stone steps into a small chamber illuminated by a chill, wintery light which filtered from leaded windows high up near the ceiling. Biggles closed the door, shutting out the squalor and obscenity of war. For a fleeting instant, time out of time, they could forget the horrors and dangers that had led to their chance meeting in this bleak, cold room, somewhere in Belgium.

Biggles went to her and gently enclosed her head in his two hands. Marie's eyes searched his face. Biggles drew her to him and pressed his lips to her smooth, wide forehead beneath the fine centre-parting. He felt a tremor run through her body.

'I thought you were dead,' Biggles murmured, his voice ragged with emotion. His eyes glittered with a strange, poignant light.

'I should have died. I wanted to many times.'

'I wish I'd known you were alive . . . but why a nunnery?'

'I had to come here,' Marie told him quietly and simply. 'These good sisters helped me – and now I help them.'

A shadow passed across Biggles' face. 'Please don't become a nun . . . yet,' he implored her.

Marie's mouth curved up in a little smile. 'I haven't . . . yet,' she said softly.

Biggles grinned. He held her shoulders, his face sobering. 'When this is over I'll come back for you. I promise.'

Marie put her arms round him and clung to him tightly, her eyes closed, her cheek pressed against the worn, cracked leather of his flying coat. She glanced up at him in sudden, swift fear.

'You must hurry! I have a map of some caves that lead to Blanchfleur. It was Blanchfleur where those bodies were discovered.'

'Do you know what it is at Blanchfleur?' queried Biggles tersely. 'What sort of weapon it is?'

'Nobody has seen it,' admitted Marie, shaking her

head. 'Only what it does. Here is the map,' she said, taking a small, folded piece of paper from the pocket of her smock and handing it to him.

It was crudely drawn, Biggles saw, but plain enough for all that: a network of caves linking the British trenches with cellars directly under the foundations of the small village of Blanchfleur. Still he had his doubts. He gnawed his lower lip, trying to quell them.

Marie saw his indecision and anxiously sought to reassure him.

'You can trust me, James. You must believe me.' There was a thin note of desperation in her voice. 'I'm not working for either side any longer. There is so much talk about this weapon – they say it turns stone to sand.' Marie gripped his hand, her knuckles white against his brown skin. 'It must not be used against men!'

Biggles' doubts evaporated under the fierceness of her conviction, the naked sincerity in her dark shining eyes. For one last time they embraced, hearts beating painfully, and then Marie broke away and ran to the door, fighting back her tears. She opened the door, not daring to look back, and quickly went out.

Standing in the doorway, Biggles watched Marie moving along the cramped aisles, pausing here and there to tend to the wounded. He squared his shoulders and strode over to where Jim and Ginger were waiting, his face quite cold and hard with implacable determination.

Biggles jerked his head. 'Right. Come on.'

They reached the door just as it flew open, crashing back on its hinges to reveal Algy and Bertie, flushed and dishevelled, revolvers in their hands.

'Germans everywhere!' panted Algy hoarsely.

'They've got us trapped,' snarled Bertie through gritted teeth.

Biggles drew his service revolver and led his team to the nearest window, where they took up positions, crouching below the line of sight. Flattening himself against the wall, Biggles inched sideways and peered out. The place was crawling with them. The Huns had taken over every vantage point and available scrap of cover, encircling the convent in a ring of steel. Machine-guns had been set up, positioned to give a converging angle of fire on every exit. Everywhere Biggles looked, weapons and helmets gleamed dully in the weak sunshine.

Bertie screwed his monocle more firmly into his eye. 'They came from all sides,' he declared, sounding puzzled and more than a bit miffed.

Algy nodded his agreement. 'They must have had the whole convent under surveillance,' he conjectured grimly.

Ginger whirled round. 'We've bloody well been betrayed,' he muttered darkly, glaring at Marie.

The girl stood rigidly, fists knotted at her sides. Her face was deathly white. She caught Biggles stricken glance and shook her head in dumb eloquent denial. He stared at her with narrowed eyes and clamped his jaw, turning his head away with barely concealed disgust.

'We can't make a scrap of it in here, not with these people,' Biggles told the others in a low voice, indicating the nuns and their wounded charges. 'We'll get outside and then look for an opportunity. Who's got a hanky?'

Bertie produced a silk monogrammed handkerchief. This was tied to a bronze candle-holder and dangled through the window. There was a stir of activity outside. Footsteps rang sharply on the flagged courtyard, and a harsh guttural voice barked in German:

'Out! Out! Hands up!'

Biggles turned to Jim, and with a terse, 'Stay here,' beckoned to the others and led them outside, hands held high.

At once they were surrounded by armed soldiers in field grey and hustled to the centre of the courtyard. Their revolvers were taken and they were thoroughly searched for more weapons. Finding none, the soldiers fell back, rifles cocked and at the ready. A blond officer in a flat cap strutted up and stood with booted legs apart, hands on hips.

'Any others inside?' he demanded menacingly.

Biggles met the officer's arrogant stare levelly. There was only one way of dealing with Prussians of his ilk.

'We're the lot,' replied Biggles coolly. He raised a negligent eyebrow towards the convent. 'Only women and children left.'

The officer didn't care for Biggles' attitude, which didn't worry Biggles one jot. The air was his element, where duels were fought on equal terms, with honour and respect for one's adversary, soaring aloft in the wide blue ocean of sky amidst tumbling white icebergs of clouds; not grubbing down here on the leaden earth, in the muck and the mire, dealing with stiff-necked bullies and cowards who were at their best terrorising the weak and defenceless.

Seeing that Biggles wasn't the type to be brow-beaten or intimidated, the blond officer turned sullenly on his heel and strode towards the chapel, flanked by a dozen men.

From inside the chapel, Jim had witnessed Biggles' attempt to divert the enemy's attention and thus prevent them from entering. But now, watching the officer heading purposefully this way, Jim realised he was in one hell of a fix. It was too late to hide. And hide where? He possessed no weapon. Dressed as he was in this ridiculous nun's habit he would be picked out immediately. Then what? As an American not in uniform, would they take him to be a spy? Jim's blood ran cold as he remembered what they did to spies in wartime . . .

There and then. On the spot. No trial. No mercy.

The officer kicked open the door and his shadow fell on the flagged floor. Jim stumbled back, his mind blank with panic. Marie was suddenly beside him. In one swift smooth movement she planted a huge white winged bonnet on his head. As the officer came in, Jim hid his hands inside the voluminous grey sleeves and bowed his head meekly under the shadow of the nun's hat.

At a brusque command, the soldiers fanned out and pointed their rifles at the nuns, standing in small huddled groups. Taking his time, the officer stood back on his heels and surveyed the room. His gaze came to rest on Jim. His eyes narrowed. He strutted over and peered closely into Jim's face. Jim kept his eyes demurely lowered to the ground. After several moments of puzzled scrutiny the officer sniffed, grunted, and turned his back. Then he said something sharply in German, and without taking any further interest in the proceedings marched to the door and went out.

Jim's shoulders sagged and he released a long sigh of relief.

But too soon, it transpired – for with shouts and much gesturing with their rifles the soldiers rounded up the nuns, with Jim and Marie in the centre of the silent, frightened group, and herded them outside into the courtyard.

There they were pushed and prodded into line against a wall. From under the winged bonnet Jim saw that Biggles and his friends were receiving the same treatment. Jim's fear that he was about to be shot returned. But surely not the nuns? No, he refused to believe it.

The same dread thought had crossed Biggles' mind.

Standing shoulder-to-shoulder with Algy, Bertie and Ginger, their backs to the wall, faced at point-blank range by the grey line of German infantry, his mind was racing as he desperately sought a way out. Their revolvers had been taken and there were too many to take on even in a fair fight. The situation looked hopeless.

Biggles glanced up keenly at the muted, purring sound of an engine, and moments later a large and luxuriously appointed open touring car with red leather seats, gleaming dark green coachwork, and pennants flying, swept grandly through the arched gate and pulled up in the courtyard with a sigh of brakes.

A corporal ran forward to open the rear door, and from the car stepped a tall, ramrod-straight, sardonically handsome figure in the grey uniform of the *Jagdstaffeln*, with red piping, gold-thread epaulettes, and two rows of gilt buttons. The Iron Cross and other decorations were displayed, in German military fashion, in a vertical row down the left-hand side of his tunic.

Biggles caught his breath. This was the man with whom he had fought many duels in the air. But never before had he come face to face with his adversary – this time without his iron mask.

8

VON STALHEIN PROPOSES
A TOAST

Had it been up to Bertie, he would have willingly
throttled the blond officer with his bare hands. Fortu-
nately perhaps, Algy and Ginger were there to res-
train him, knowing they were powerless to do
anything as Biggles was dragged from the line by three
soldiers and frog-marched away. The three flyers
could only glower at the officer in charge, silently
vowing to make him pay for such brutish behaviour
should the opportunity present itself.

As for Biggles, he feared the worst. But he was in
for something of a surprise. Instead of being thrust in
front of a firing squad he was taken to the private
study of the Mother Superior, on the far side of the
convent, and left there alone to stew for several
minutes. What was in the wind? Biggles racked his
brains as he waited, but admitted to himself to being
completely in the dark.

Eventually, the door opened and in strode the
imposingly tall figure of his arch enemy wearing the
uniform of the *Jagdstaffeln*, the crack fighter squadrons of the German Imperial Air Corps. A soldier

entered behind him, bearing something under a white cloth, and stood obediently just inside the door.

The German flyer came to a halt, removed his cap, and tucked it smartly under his arm. His eyes were a piercing icy blue, and a slightly mocking smile hovered about his thin lips.

Quite at ease, despite his predicament, Biggles eyed the other with an assured air that bordered on nonchalance.

'The famous Biggles,' were the German's opening words, spoken in excellent English with only the faintest trace of an accent. 'We meet at last.'

'Hauptmann Erich von Stalhein,' Biggles responded in his turn.

Von Stalhein went taut as a bowstring, snapped his heels together, and bowed stiffly from the waist.

Biggles raised his eyebrows, a hint of amusement lurking on his frank, open features. 'Haven't you forgotten your iron mask?' he inquired banteringly.

Von Stalhein ignored the remark and clicked his fingers. The soldier stepped forward, and swept off the white cloth to reveal a bottle of the finest champagne and two crystal goblets on a silver tray. When the wine had been poured, von Stalhein offered a glass to Biggles and raised his own glass in a toast.

'To the gods of war!' he barked.

'To peace,' said Biggles quietly. He tasted the champagne and nodded his approval. 'Incidentally, how did you know I was here?'

'Some of our infantrymen saw a plane land beyond the bridge just after dawn. I knew immediately there was only one pilot foolhardy enough to take such a risk.'

Von Stalhein smiled thinly and arched an eyebrow.
'A great pity. I would have much preferred to kill
you in the air rather than by firing squad.'

'Perhaps. But this way you're far less likely to botch
the job,' murmured Biggles sardonically.

The German fighter ace stiffened as if slapped
across the face, and the blood drained from his
cheeks. With a sweep of his hand he gestured the
soldiers forward, who pinioned Biggles' arms behind
his back and frog-marched him from the room.

* * *

Head bowed under the winged bonnet, Jim watched
Biggles return to the courtyard under armed guard,
and thought he saw a mixture of steely defiance and at
the same time quiet desperation in the airman's eyes.
Close behind came von Stalhein, who paused to have
a word in the blond officer's ear.

The officer nodded brusquely and called his men to
attention. They began to form a line facing the prison-
ers, working the bolts of their weapons in readiness.
Biggles exchanged a grim look with his comrades.
They had been in some tight spots, but none tighter
than this. His mind was racing, searching desperately
for a chink that might save them; he didn't have long,
minutes at the most.

Despondently, Jim hunched himself deeper into
the grey habit, thrusting his hands into the long
slit-like pockets of the robe. His fingers touched a
hard, square object with a curved metal end. He took
it out and looked down at it, concealed in the folds of
the habit.

His battery-powered electric shaver. He'd pocketed it earlier on and completely forgotten about it.

Jim acted immediately and instinctively. Flicking the switch, he tossed the shaver right at the front of the line of guards, yelling 'Grenade!' at the top of his voice.

For a second or two the guards froze, staring with bulging eyes at the mysterious buzzing object, and then there was a mad scrambling panic as they leapt out of the way, scattering in all directions, tripping over their rifles and each other in total disarray.

Taking advantage of the confusion, Biggles spun round, wrapped his arm round von Stalhein's neck, and yanked the German's Mauser from its holster. The others waded in, fists flying, sending half a dozen guards crashing to the ground and grabbing their rifles.

Falling back, the blond officer and the rest of his men regrouped, facing the four British flyers across the courtyard in a tense confrontation. With one arm locked across von Stalhein's throat, Biggles cocked the hammer on the Mauser and pressed the muzzle to the German's temple. The blond officer held up his hand, cautioning his men to hold their fire.

'You'll be the first to sprout wings, von Stalhein,' grated Biggles through his teeth. 'Tell them to drop their guns.'

Von Stalhein hesitated, then barked out an order, knowing he had no alternative. As the blond officer and his men dropped their weapons, Ginger darted forward and collected them, dumping them in a corner.

Biggles glanced over his shoulder and gave Jim a wry grin.

'*Merci*, Sister. You'd better come with us.'

Algy and Bertie were already heading for the staff car. Jim picked up his skirts and followed. On the way he coquettishly winked at the blond officer, who stared at him in dumbfounded amazement.

Backing towards the car with his hostage, Biggles spared the last look for Marie, who lifted her head and smiled in sad farewell.

Algy started the engine of the car as Bertie jumped in beside him, Ginger tumbling into the back seat. Jim climbed on to the running board and hung on as Algy released the handbrake and started to move off. Dragging von Stalhein with him, Biggles leapt on to the other running board.

'I'm not going to put a bullet in your head, because that's not the way we do business,' snapped Biggles, nostrils flared, and with that he whipped his arm away, and, giving him a kick for good measure, sent the tall elegant figure tumbling in the dust.

Algy pressed the accelerator to the floor and the huge open car surged forward powerfully. Jim gave a terrified yell as he lost his grip. He teetered on the running board and then he too went down, rolling head over heels, enveloped in flapping grey skirts. He was up in an instant, running after the car.

'Fire!' Fire!'

Von Stalhein had scrambled to his feet and was yelling hoarsely at the guards, his face a livid mask.

Shots whistled past Jim's ear as he stretched out his hand to Ginger, who was hanging out of the back of the car, straining to reach him. Their fingers touched. Jim got a firmer grip. And at that moment the grey skirts wrapped themselves round his ankles and he tripped and went sprawling full-length onto the rutted track, the car speeding off in a cloud of blue smoke.

Flat out and badly winded, Jim watched it go with despairing eyes, ducking his head as more shots kicked up dirt all around him. Boots pounded along the track. But Jim had ceased to pay them any heed. He was staring instead at his hands. He was suddenly wearing a pair of shimmering yellow gloves . . .

The nearest guard got to within ten feet of the figure lying prone on the ground – which appeared to be covered from head to toe in a peculiar pulsing light – when it rolled itself up into a flickering yellow ball and vanished.

* * *

'Jim?' Debbie frowned worriedly and tapped on the door of 1231. She tensed, one hand holding the collar of her silver fox fur close to her throat. That noise again. This time a muffled thump followed by a mangled cry. 'Are you all right?'

She stared at the door, and then glanced at Chuck, who gave a ponderous shrug, pulling down the corners of his mouth like a disgruntled trout. He was still clutching *Diseases of the Mind* in his hand. In fact, on the flight over he'd carried it like a talisman, as if it might ward off evil spirits.

'Jim?' Debbie said again, more frightened than worried now.

The door opened a crack, and Debbie pushed it with her gloved hand. 'Can I come in?'

There was a deep and sombre groan, and then, faintly but distinctly, Jim's voice said, 'Can you wait a minute?'

Debbie couldn't. She was beside herself with worry. She pushed harder and the door swung open to reveal a nun in a long grey habit and huge white winged bonnet. The nun had Jim's face. Debbie's jaw sagged open. Jim grinned weakly, then his face fell as Chuck stuck his head into view.

'Hi, Jim.'

Debbie stumbled mechanically into the room with Chuck close behind, his horrified whisper rasping in her ear. 'It's worse than I thought . . . he's become a religious transvestite!'

Chuck's eyes popped out of his head as he spotted the sub-machine-gun under the chair. He swallowed hard, digging Debbie frantically in the ribs. 'A transvestite bank robber! That's not even in the book!'

Debbie tried to make it sound casual, even conversational, but her voice was limp with shock as she asked tremulously, 'Why are you wearing that dress . . . and that hat?'

Glancing upwards, realising what he still had on his head, Jim whipped the bonnet off. He tossed it aside and backed away, raising both hands. 'Now listen, both of you.' He cleared his throat. 'There's a very good explanation for all this . . .'

Debbie slowly folded her arms, looking like a svelte fashion model in her full-length fur coat, and peered suspiciously round the room, as if checking it out for further mind-boggling surprises. 'I sure hope so,' she murmured doubtfully.

The phone rang. Grateful for the distraction, Jim snatched up the receiver from the bedside table. 'Yes, this is Mr Ferguson in 1231.'

'A Colonel Raymond called, sir,' reported the desk

clerk. 'He asked you to go over to see him immediately.'

'Fine. Thank you.'

Jim hung up, nodding to himself in grim resolve. Events were speeding up; there was action to be taken. But first things first. He strode across to Chuck and jabbed his finger into the flabby chest.

'Out!'

Chuck opened his mouth to protest, holding up the book in self-defence, and found himself being propelled rapidly across the room, through the door and into the corridor before he had time to draw breath.

'Okay, Jim, I can take a hint,' he bleated as the door slammed in his childishly hurt face.

Jim turned back to see Debbie pulling out the sub-machine-gun from under the chair. On her face was a horrified mixture of bewilderment and alarm. 'Jim, what is this? What's going on?'

'Debbie – I know this looks bad,' Jim conceded calmly, taking the weapon from her and shoving it in a drawer. 'But I'm going to take you to somebody who can explain everything. Just as soon as I change clothes. We've got to hurry!'

For a blank moment Debbie simply stared at him uncertainly, biting her lower lip. He looked so ridiculous and pathetic, standing there in the nun's grey habit reaching down to his ankles, an imploring look in his eyes. The next moment she was in his arms, holding him tight.

* * *

Chuck mooched disconsolately through the hotel lobby, still smarting from Jim's rough-and-ready treatment of a close buddy. Not to mention his ingratitude! Chuck scowled. He only wanted to help the guy. Jim was obviously deep in some kind of psychiatric trouble. He'd cracked up under the strain. Psychosis Trauma Syndrome, like the book said.

He waddled towards the bar, intent on consoling himself with a drink or two, or three, when he was suddenly struck by a bright idea. A brilliant idea. Turning about, he hurried over to one of the phones in the lobby and called the hotel operator.

Clutching the book to his chest, as if about to deliver a lecture to the institute of Freudian Studies, Chuck swelled up importantly as she came on the line.

'This is Dr Charles Winthrop Dinsmore in the lobby,' he began in a weighty, pompous tone. 'I'm a psychiatrist from New York. One of my patients is staying with you and I need some help with him. If you would please arrange for an ambulance, I would be most grateful. He's in Room 1231. Oh, and a couple of good strong attendants,' he added as an afterthought.

'Why, is your patient dangerous?' the operator inquired worriedly.

'Ha-ha, of course not.' Chuck laughed jovially, waving such a suggestion aside. 'He's just confused. He's wearing a nun's dress, and has a gun – '

'Did you say – a *gun*?'

Automatically the operator's hand jumped to a button on the panel in front of her. She pressed it decisively. Above her blonde head a buzzer sounded and a red light began to flash.

9

DANGEROUS WORK

With Debbie trotting alongside to keep up with him, Jim strode briskly along Pepys Street, crossed over, and turned right into Coopers Row, all the while casting sharp glances over his shoulder as if afraid of being followed. There was a biting, blustery wind, and Jim was glad of his zippered woollen windcheater and the thick tartan scarf knotted under his chin. Glad to be back in warm decent clothes, period.

'Why'd we come out the back way?' Debbie panted as they came into Trinity Square. Her eyes sparkled and her cheeks were flushed with the cold air and the exertion.

'I didn't want to take Chuck,' answered Jim shortly. 'Things are crazy enough.' He looked intently to left and right, and set off purposefully across the square. A tug hooted mournfully on the river beyond Tower Hill.

'Where are we going?'

'Trust me.'

Debbie caught his arm, slowing him down as they came to some green wrought-iron railings enclosing empty flower beds and a patch of tired grass. Fumes from the circling traffic formed a pretty, yet lethal, blue mist.

'Jim, won't you please tell me *what's going on*?'

Jim stopped and faced her. There was a guarded look in his eyes as he took hold of her shoulders, almost as if it was himself he had to convince and not her.

'Okay, Debbie. Nobody ever believes it, but here goes.'

Jim took a breath and tightened his lips. 'I've been falling through a hole in time. Going back to 1917.'

He watched her face closely, searching for signs of incredulity, or laughter, or fear maybe, but Debbie was gazing back at him with total seriousness, not a hint of disbelief in her clear, wide hazel eyes. Then she nodded, just once.

'Yes? Go on.'

'You believe me?' Jim said, delight creeping slowly across his face.

'If you say so, Jim, then I believe you,' said Debbie meekly.

Jim laughed with relief and hugged her to him. He kissed her on the nose and they continued walking, arm in arm, across the square in the direction of Tower Hill.

'I keep going back to World War I,' Jim went on, eager now to unburden himself to someone, 'where I'm helping this guy named Biggles find and destroy this German secret weapon . . .'

He was still talking animatedly as they turned a corner and came onto the Northern Approach to Tower Bridge, the two massive stone towers outlined against the leaden sky. There was drizzle in the air, sweeping in from the broad grey river.

'So that's it. I fell out of the car and – bang – I'm back here again. And that's why I was wearing that nun's outfit.'

He grinned down at her, shaking his head. 'Pretty crazy story, huh?'

Debbie nodded slowly. 'I'm just glad Chuck didn't hear it,' she said, glancing up at him with a frown.

* * *

Chuck drained his glass as the announcement came over the public address system, requesting 'Dr Dinsmore' to go along to reception where a message was awaiting him. Chuck hurried from the bar and bustled over to the clerk behind the desk.

'I'm Dr Dinsmore.'

'The doorman has a parcel for you, sir,' smiled the clerk.

Chuck rubbed his chins in consternation. Who could have sent him a parcel? He shrugged and headed back through the lobby to the main entrance, pushing through the glass doors. The doorman was standing on the pavement, having just despatched a couple in a taxi.

'I'm Dr Dinsmore. You have something for me?'

'I certainly do, sir,' said the doorman, touching his cap and sliding a hand inside the tunic of his royal blue uniform with the fancy gold braid. The hand re-appeared, holding a .45 magnum revolver, which he pointed at the second button down on Chuck's bulging overcoat. 'You're under arrest.'

Chuck goggled at him.

There was a squeal of tyres and a police car with blue lights flashing raced up and screeched to a halt on rocking springs. The rear door was flung open and Chuck was bundled inside between two burly plain-clothes men. With a supercharged roar the car shot off down the street, a numbed and petrified Chuck wedged in the back seat.

* * *

'Jim, listen please.'

Debbie had stopped. She stood resolutely on the pavement, huddled up in her fur coat, the wind chasing wisps of hair over her forehead. Jim turned to look at her, hands thrust deep into his side pockets. He waited.

'I'm not saying I don't believe you about going into the past and everything . . .' Debbie hesitated. She plunged on, a little recklessly. 'But will you promise me one thing? Will you try to get some help?'

'Sure. That's exactly why we're going to the bridge,' Jim assured her cheerfully.

Debbie shook her head angrily. 'Jim, forget the bridge nonsense. I mean real help. Psychiatric help.'

Jim took his hands out of his pockets, his face stony. 'I thought you said you believed me,' he muttered coldly.

'I do – I mean . . . I'm sure all this is very real to you . . .'

Debbie avoided his eyes. Jim went on staring at her, his dark brows drawn together in bitter resentment. Then his expression changed. A look of horrified panic suffused his face as an ominous peal of thunder crashed directly above their heads.

'Come on! There isn't much time!' Jim cried, grabbing Debbie's arm and pulling her towards the bridge.

They hadn't gone more than a dozen paces when there came the wail of sirens, and glancing over his shoulder Jim saw a police car turn the corner practically on two wheels and race along the Northern Approach towards them. In the back seat he could see a pale blob of a face and a wildly gesticulating flabby hand.

Jim stopped dead in his tracks. Everything was happening too fast. Already it was too late. He looked down despairingly at his hands and saw blue sparks flashing between his fingertips. The force-field was sending long crackling electric feelers up his arms.

'Jim, what's wrong?' Debbie screamed, her voice almost drowned by a *boom*! of thunder that shook the pavement under their feet. She ran to him, clinging desperately on to his arm, and Jim wrenched himself free.

'Get away from me!' he yelled, frantically pushing her away.

But Debbie wouldn't let go. She hung on to him as a bolt of charged electrons leapt from Jim's body and curled back on itself in a glittering arc, enveloping them both in a lambent halo of intensely bright light. There was another ear-splitting crack of thunder and then –

Nothing.

* * *

The sky was the same, unrelieved grey with dark scudding clouds, Debbie saw with relief, blinking her

ALEX HYDE WHITE as Jim at the Celebrity Dinners launch party

PETER CUSHING as Colonel Raymond, Biggles' boss

NEIL DICKSON as Biggles

In the trenches

Biggles' first meeting with Debbie (FIONA HUTCHISON), in the trenches

Jim time warps back to the Belgian convent

Biggles, Jim and Debbie held captive by the Germans

FRANCESCA GONSHAW as Mari is held at the convent

Biggles and his chums face the firing-squad

The secret weapon is destroyed

Biggles and Jim take off in the helicopter

Sunset – the helicopter flies to the rescue

Biggles thanks his chums

eyes open. Then she looked about her and saw that nothing else was. In place of Tower Bridge – a wall of mud, topped with barbed-wire. No pavement under her feet; instead slatted wooden duckboards sinking into the thick watery ooze. And the sounds had changed too – from tugs hooting on the river to the distant but unmistakable rattle of machine-guns.

It was okay, she told herself calmly, she'd wake up soon. Any minute now.

Jim was half-crouching, peering alertly to left and right along the narrow trench, which was shored up with sandbags and beams of rotted timber. A pall of oily black smoke drifted overhead, obscuring the sky like a gigantic reaching hand. Jim's nostrils crinkled at the acrid stench. He started, jerked his head up, hearing a sound that had now become for him dreadfully familiar – a dull thud followed by the steadily rising shriek of a mortar shell as it dropped towards them over no-man's land.

'Get down!'

Jim flung Debbie against the wall of mud and shielded her body with his as the mortar screamed down and exploded on the lip of the trench, showering them with dirt and stones. Half-deafened by the blast, his limbs rubbery with shock, Jim was struggling weakly to rise, earth and debris cascading down his back, when his shoulder was taken in a firm grip and he was hauled to his feet.

A pair of steady grey eyes graven with tiny lines at the corners gazed at him incredulously out of a grimy, smoke-blackened face.

'Good God!' exclaimed Biggles in astonishment. 'Ferguson!'

Jim shook his head to clear it and experimented with a grin.

'Damn me, it's the American chap!' declared Bertie, peering over Biggles' shoulder, the monocle as firmly in place as the Rock of Gibraltar.

Algy's tall figure hove into view, his officer's cap set at a rakish angle, and behind him came Ginger, his freckles and fair colouring disguised under a layer of dried mud.

In fact all four looked as if they'd slogged it to hell and back, and fought every inch of the way.

Biggles, still in flying-kit, carried a snub-nosed sub-machine-gun cradled in his arm. A nest of satchel bombs was slung over one shoulder, a gas-mask case over the other. The others too, Jim noted, were all fully equipped with a variety of small arms, cartridge belts and portable munitions. Altogether a formidable fighting team, on the ground as well as in the air.

Jim stooped to rescue Debbie from the bottom of the trench, lifting her up and brushing off the dirt and mud as best he could. She was pale, trembling, still dazed, and her elegant silver fox fur was in a sorry state.

The four airmen stood rivetted to the spot, gaping at her in stunned amazement.

'Good grief,' breathed Biggles, his jaw dropping open. 'A woman!'

'Captain Bigglesworth, this is Debbie Stevens,' said Jim, and then felt that some explanation was necessary. 'She's a – uh – nurse,' he added weakly.

Biggles took her hand and shook it courteously. 'You shouldn't be here, Miss Stevens,' he told her gravely. 'It's no place for a lady.'

Debbie winced her agreement as a mortar shell screeched overhead and exploded somewhere behind the lines with a gritty crump. Jim wrapped an arm protectively round her shoulder, hugging her close, but Debbie wasn't comforted. Besides being too damn real for her liking, this particular dream had long outstayed its welcome.

A British officer in a waterproof cape came along the trench, blowing a whistle and waving his arm. 'The enemy is advancing! Fire on my command! Fix bayonets!'

He gave a shrill blast on the whistle and all hell broke loose. Machine guns in sandbagged positions opened up with a deadly sustained hammering. Riflemen, crouched at intervals along the edge of the parapet, stood up as one man and began firing. The din was beyond human comprehension.

Still blowing his whistle, the officer moved on. The thud and whine of descending mortar shells filled the air. Gouts of earth were thrown up by the explosions, raining dirt and shrapnel down on the thin furrow of the trench. Over everything was the mingled choking smell of cordite, smoke and dust.

Biggles leaned nearer and shouted in Jim's ear. 'The Huns will be over the top any second now. Stay close behind me.'

Jim nodded to show he understood and watched Biggles and the others start to move off along the slippery duckboards. Debbie, her hands over her ears, was huddled against Jim's chest. He tried to pull her along, but she resisted.

'Come on!' Jim implored her, his fingers digging into her arm.

'I'm not moving until you stop all this nonsense!' she suddenly snarled at him, on the edge of hysteria, her eyes wild and staring, her lips bloodless.

Struggling defiantly, Debbie broke free of his embrace and staggered backwards against the wall of the trench. She felt something soft brush against her. It was a human hand, cold and white and clammy as a dead fish, protruding limply from under a pile of sandbags.

Debbie's mouth opened soundlessly, and then her scream joined the bedlam of machine-guns and rifle shots and mortar shells going on all around her. As if drained by the sudden release of tension, she sagged weakly and fell into Jim's arms. Supporting her round the waist, Jim set off after Biggles and the others.

Thirty yards further on, Biggles had reached the connecting trench he had been seeking, running at an angle to the main trench. He waved the others on and waited anxiously for Jim and Debbie to catch up. Led by a sergeant, a squad of Tommies went past him in a crouching run. One by one, like a row of marionettes, their heads wobbled round as their glassy eyes took in the sight of the young girl in the fur coat stumbling along the trench. The blank incredulity on their weary faces was matched by Debbie's own, who still couldn't accept the evidence of her own senses.

Biggles turned briskly and led the way along the smaller side trench to what at first glance appeared to be the entrance to a mine, excavated out of the trench wall. The sides were shored up with timber planking and sandbags. There was a bustle of activity, with soldiers wheeling barrow-loads of earth and rubble from the tunnel, under the direction of a sapper officer.

He looked up as Biggles pushed his way forward, and saluted.

'We're connected with the cave system, sir.'

'Good man.' Biggles glanced up keenly at a fusillade of rifle fire, just beyond the rim of the trench. The enemy was closing in; time was getting desperately short. 'Better evacuate your chaps,' he ordered curtly.

The officer ran to it, clearing his men from the entrance. Then Biggles gave Algy the nod, who at once darted into the dark mouth of the tunnel, Bertie and Ginger close behind. Biggles indicated to Jim that he and Debbie should follow.

Jim gripped Debbie's hand, but she drew back. Her eyes were shocked and vacant.

'Jim, tell me this is some kind of terrible dream,' she mumbled emptily. 'Tell me – '

'I told you,' rasped Jim through clenched teeth, 'I keep going back to 1917. And anything I'm holding – or is holding me – goes along.'

Debbie shook her head numbly.

'Take me back. Let's go back . . .'

Biggles waved them frantically towards the entrance as heads in spiked helmets started to appear on the skyline. 'Into the tunnel,' he snapped, losing patience. 'And hurry!'

'No, Jim – I'm not going in there!' Debbie screamed as Jim struggled with her.

A stick grenade twirled lazily through the air and landed at Debbie's feet. Jim sprang forward, scooped it up, and lobbed it back with all his strength in the direction of the advancing enemy. There was a vivid orange flash as it exploded in mid-air, and a strangled cry just out of sight over the ridge. Firing from the hip, Biggles sprayed short bursts to keep the enemy at bay.

But already more figures, dozens of them, were appearing over the top, some wearing gas masks with great bulbous eyes and long rubber snouts, resembling a deformed species of elephant. Debbie took one look at these monstrosities and didn't need any more persuading. She ran for the tunnel, Jim diving in behind her.

This left Biggles to conclude the final act.

With incredible coolness, the young airman took one of the satchel charges from its pouch, lit the fuse, and slowly backed into the tunnel entrance. Holding the satchel bomb with its fizzing fuse in his hands, he counted off the seconds, waiting for precisely the right moment.

Boots thudded down and soon the trench was swarming with the advance wave of German troops. While the rest gave covering fire, two of them advanced into the tunnel, Biggles slowly retreating one step at a time.

Finally, judging the moment to be right, Biggles gave a terse shout of 'Run!' over his shoulder and flung the smoking satchel bomb at the feet of the advancing soldiers, who immediately opened fire, streaks of orange flame spitting from their rifles.

A split-second later the bomb went off, the blast blowing the soldiers out of the tunnel feet first and bringing the roof down, sealing off the entrance in an avalanche of earth and rock.

Biggles lifted his head from underneath his crossed

arms, and climbing to his feet, dusted himself down. He paused for a moment with narrowed probing eyes. Not a chink of light to be seen. And grinning into the darkness, he hitched up his shoulder packs, swung on his heel and plodded deeper into the tunnel.

10

UNDER BLANCHFLEUR

With Biggles at their head, Jim and Debbie close
behind, and Bertie, Ginger and Algy bringing up the
rear, the party trudged silently through the tunnel
blasted and dug out by the sappers under no-man's
land. Biggles carried a small but powerful battery
lantern, its beams showing the rough walls of packed
earth and clay, embedded with boulders and small
rocks, tiny slivers of flint catching the gleams of light.
His comrades carried Air Corps-issue torches, their
pencil-thin beams slicing through the darkness.

Continuously, from up above, they could hear the
dull reverberating boom of the blanket bombardment, and the heavy thud of the German artillery
returning fire. When a shell landed close, the tunnel
shuddered under the impact, sending down a thick
cloud of dust and a rattle of small stones. Jim kept
glancing fearfully at the ceiling, expecting it to cave in
at any moment. Debbie hadn't uttered a sound for
some time, and Jim wondered if she was still in shock
or had come to accept the reality of the situation.
There was little else she could do, he reasoned. This,
for now, was their reality, and they were stuck with it.

The further into the tunnel they went, the narrower it became, the walls more uneven, and lower, so they had to stoop slightly.

Ahead, Biggles' dark hunched shape was silhouetted against the glare of the lantern. Jim had only a vague idea of the aim of the mission. Under the circumstances there hadn't been time for a briefing.

'Hey, Biggles, hold it a second,' he called out after a while, his voice sounding flat and muffled in the confined space.

'Mind telling me the plan?' Jim asked, as the group caught up and clustered round the battery lantern. The bright light made empty black sockets of their eyes. Bertie's monocle flashed like a dusty silver coin.

Biggles pulled a folded sheet of paper from his pocket and opened it out. 'We're going into the caves under the village of Blanchfleur – using this map that Marie gave me. We've got to find out what kind of weapon it is.' Stern-faced, he jerked his thumb at the ceiling, towards the heavy rumble of guns and the crunch of falling shells. 'This is the big offensive. I think it'll be only hours before they use the weapon.

He glanced apologetically at Debbie. 'Sorry I had to bring you along, Miss Stevens, but it was either that or the Germans.'

Debbie smiled wanly and huddled closer to Jim.

Time being of the essence, the party quickly moved on, Biggles referring constantly to his map now to locate the point where the sappers' tunnel linked up to the caves. Ten minutes later he found it, the beam of the lantern revealing a round jagged opening branching off from the main tunnel. The others came up and shone their torches into the pitch-black hole.

Walls of rock gleamed wetly, dripping with moisture. Parts of the roof had fallen in, and the uneven, slippery floor was strewn with debris and shards of stone. It looked far from inviting.

'This is it,' pronounced Biggles in a clipped tone, putting the map away. 'The start of the cave system.' He glanced round the circle, his face set and sober. 'In we go.'

If the tunnel had been bad, this dank-smelling jagged fissure, with sharp edges of rock poking dangerously from the roof, was even worse. Debbie clung tightly to Jim's arm as they picked their way carefully over the rough, littered floor.

The bombardment continued above their heads, seeming louder than before, and when an explosion shook the walls and brought down part of the roof with a clatter of shattered rock, Debbie screamed and covered her head with her hands.

'Oh my God! We're going to be buried alive!'

Another explosion – louder still and even closer – rocked the tunnel, bringing down more of the roof.

Debbie turned her face blindly to the wall, crouching to shield herself, and a partly decomposed body dressed in rags, its skull leering at her in a grimace of death, detached itself from the wall and fell on top of her, a skeletal hand dropping on to her shoulder with a bony rattle.

Debbie shuddered repulsively and covered her mouth, too benumbed by shock now even to scream. Jim pulled her away from the deathly embrace while Biggles stepped forward and calmly pushed the rotting corpse back into its resting place.

'It's some kind of hallucinatory experience, right?'

Debbie mumbled into Jim's shoulder, trying to find a rational explanation. She looked up at him, blinking brightly. 'Those mushrooms Chuck and I had on the plane!'

Jim held her tightly as they stumbled on.

A short while later Biggles came to a halt and scrutinised the way ahead with the lantern. Here the tunnel divided into two, with a smaller passage branching off to the left. He consulted the map as the others gathered round, and then put it way with a brief, decisive nod.

'The spur to Blanchfleur should be another thirty yards along here.' Biggles indicated the main tunnel. 'Bertie, come with me. We'll do a recce. Ginger, you and Algy scout that one. Jim, you and –' Biggles lifted a quizzical eyebrow ' – and the nurse wait here.'

Bertie handed his torch to Jim and moved off after Biggles, while Algy and Ginger set off to explore the smaller tunnel.

Exhausted, Debbie slumped against the wall and closed her eyes, her face a pale oval in the dim light of the pencil-thin beam. Jim squatted down on his haunches opposite her, feeling the damp chill of the tunnel seeping into his bones.

'This can't get any worse,' murmured Debbie wearily, half to herself, and opened her eyes cautiously as a furtive scraping sound came to her ears. Scrambling to her feet, she stared in disbelief at a spade breaking through the wall near the roof, and then at the face of a German soldier, equally as shocked, peering through the hole. A beam of light flicked on, catching her full in its glare.

'*Mein Gott – Ein Fräulein!*'

Precipitating a minor landslide, the soldier heaved his way through and slid down to the floor, jerking back the bolt on his rifle. Debbie pressed herself flat against the wall, biting her knuckles, as he advanced towards her. Jim's hand appeared out of the shadows, hooked the soldier in the crook of the elbow and swung him round, slamming him face-first into the wall. The soldier grunted, fumbling dazedly to raise his rifle, and Jim drove his fist into the exposed solar plexus, sending him down in a winded, crumpled heap.

There was a streak of orange flame from the hole near the roof and a shot rang out with a deafening hollow boom. Debbie gasped as the bullet gouged a chunk of rock from the wall inches above her head. Jim dragged her to the floor, desperately trying to get clear of the line of fire. Judging by the noise and activity, there were at least half-a-dozen of them. If they broke through in force, he and Debbie were sitting ducks.

A beam of light probed the tunnel, searching for them, and then the hole erupted with angry crimson flashes, pinning them down under a hail of fire that raked the walls and ricocheted like angry hornets off the bare rock.

For a dreadful, heart-stopping moment Jim thought they had broken through when he glimpsed a pair of figures scuttling in the darkness. It was with an immense surge of relief that he recognised Biggles and Bertie crouching in the shadows.

Biggles crept forward on all-fours and lobbed a fragment grenade at the hole near the roof. His aim was true. There was a blinding flash of light and the tunnel shook and reverberated with the blast, leaving a heap of smoking rubble where the hole had been.

Biggles was on his feet in a trice. 'Come on. This way,' he rapped out, with a wave of his arm.

With Algy and Ginger covering the rear, the party moved along the main tunnel, which turned and twisted through strata of rock and clay, gnarled tree roots like arthritic fingers lacing the roof and walls.

'This is it – the spur to Blanchfleur,' said Biggles, shining his lantern into a side tunnel, and at once set off, the others close behind in single file. But they hadn't gone many yards when Biggles stopped dead, his eyes narrowing at the sight of a soft green haze floating on the clammy air.

'Gas!' shouted Biggles, backing away and covering his mouth. 'Back! Get back!'

'They must be using gas shells,' observed Algy, when they had retreated to a safe distance.

Biggles nodded grimly. 'It's seeped through the ground. The cave is bound to be full of it.' He swung the square leather case round and started to unbuckle it. 'Masks on!'

His companions pulled out their gas masks, large cumbersome affairs made of stiffened canvas with a glass viewing plate, and put them on, clipping the flexible rubber breathing tubes to canisters on their belts. Biggles was about to slip the straps over his head when he paused, noticing Jim's scared expression.

'Where are your gas masks?'

'We don't have any,' Jim confessed, swallowing hard.

Biggles pulled off his mask and handed it to

Debbie. 'Take mine.' He turned to Bertie. 'Give Ferguson your scarf.'

Bertie unwound his long white scarf and passed it to Jim.

'You and I will use scarf filters,' Biggles told him curtly. 'Standard procedure when you don't have a gas mask.'

Jim watched, goggle-eyed, as Biggles removed his scarf and unfastened his fly.

'The gas is neutralised by uric acid,' explained Biggles calmly. 'Do as I do. Turn your back, please, Miss.'

Debbie stared, mesmerised, as Jim followed Biggles' example and unzipped his fly.

'Jim, what are you doing?'

She coloured and suddenly spun round to face the wall as the realisation of what they were doing dawned on her. A moment or two later Biggles looked critically at Jim's scarf, shaking his head sadly.

'It's the best I can do,' Jim apologised weakly.

'Keep it tight against your mouth and nose.' Biggles demonstrated, wrapping his own scarf around the lower half of his face and tying it in a knot behind his neck. Jim copied him, screwing up his eyes and wrinkling his nose in distaste.

Debbie was holding the mask and looking at it almost with horror. 'I don't like things covering my face – ' she began, and broke off into a spasm of coughing and spluttering as a wave of gas wafted over them. Quickly she pulled the mask on, Ginger helping her to adjust the straps.

Biggles glanced once round the group, satisfying himself that they were all prepared, and then with a terse, 'All right. Come on,' dropped to his knees and started crawling through the gas-filled cave.

* * *

A makeshift ladder – two warped lengths of timber with odd scraps of wood hammered in to form rungs – led steeply upwards into a narrow board-walled shaft. Biggles placed his foot on the bottom rung and shone the lantern upwards.

'This is it, we're under Blanchfleur,' he announced with some satisfaction, his voice slightly muffled by the scarf swathing his mouth.

There was a general air of relief that they had achieved their objective. But Biggles was still vigilant, as was made plain when he checked the magazine on his sub-machine-gun before starting the climb. In fact the mission had only just begun.

A minute or so later he was pushing aside a heap of rubble and splintered wood as he emerged from the shaft into the wreckage of a house, almost completely demolished by shellfire. Half a roof tilted down at a crazy angle, precariously supported by broken walls and shattered beams. A thick layer of dust and debris lay over everything.

Biggles unwound the scarf and sucked in a lungful of air, then helped Debbie out of the shaft. Straightening up, she tore the gas mask from her face, closing her eyes in a silent, heartfelt prayer and breathing in deeply. Fresh air had never tasted so sweet.

Jim climbed out, followed by the others, all of them taking a few moments to clear their heads while Biggles kept a sharp lookout through the broken shell of the building. A few flakes of snow whirled down from a sky that was a monotonous dirty grey. It was bitterly cold.

With their gas masks stowed away and weapons at the ready, the party moved cautiously through the rubble-filled streets. Not a single building remained intact. Windows gaped emptily like the eyes of skulls. Crumbling walls formed a tumbled, jagged skyline. Small smoky fires guttered here and there amongst the ruins, but there were no signs of life, not even the barking of a stray dog.

The small town of Blanchfleur had been utterly devastated.

Standing in the partial shelter of what had been a two-storey building, Biggles surveyed the scene with grim, angry eyes. This was the result of no ordinary bombardment; the Boches had deliberately chosen the town for some kind of experiment – as a target or testing-ground.

'Looks like this place was nuked,' Jim told Debbie in a low voice as they both gazed round in awe.

'*Nuked*?' exclaimed Debbie in a loud, puzzled voice. 'I thought you said we were in 1917?'

Biggles raised his hand for silence, and then glanced at them sharply, frowning.

'What's "nuked"?'

'It's American slang,' said Jim, catching Debbie's eye. 'It means . . . to over-react.'

Biggles nodded thoughtfully. With a wave of his gloved hand he urged them forward, picking their way along the rubble-strewn street in single file. Eventually they came to what was left of the main square. The ruined town hall, one hand remaining on the shattered face of the clock, presided over an eerie wasteland of broken-backed houses and shops with their glass fronts blown out – and something else too. Something in the centre of the square that halted all six of them in their tracks and made them stare with puzzled, incredulous eyes.

'What the hell is that?' inquired Jim blankly, of no one in particular.

At first glance it looked like an igloo. It was a low, semi-spherical structure made up of whitish, almost translucent blocks, fairly wide at the base, rising to a smooth domed top. Portholes of thick glass were spaced around the circumference, and the fine outline of what appeared to be a small door or hatch with rounded corners.

'Shouldn't be surprised to see some Eskimos,' ventured Bertie, blowing a plume of misty breath into the air. 'Damn well cold enough.'

'Let's take a look, shall we?'

Biggles stepped forward warily, motioning the others to advance but to keep a respectable distance from the strange object.

As they approached in a slowly converging circle, Algy spotted something off to the left, and uttered a sharp word of warning. Everyone paused and swivelled round to look, their faces stony. A row of figures were tied to stakes, their bodies slack, heads slumped forward. They wore khaki battledress and round helmets. They were British Tommies.

'Swine!' Algy ground out, disgust showing in the hard lines of his face.

Biggles turned back abruptly to the business in hand. Nothing could be done now to help those poor blighters.

Jim had knelt and was examining the igloo-shaped construction curiously. The curved, closely jointed blocks gave off a hollow clunk as he rapped them with his knuckles. He glanced up at the others.

'These are ceramic – like the tiles on the Space Shuttle.'

'What on earth are you talking about?' muttered Bertie perplexedly, tugging at his moustache.

'What I'm saying,' Jim explained patiently, 'is that these tiles are made to withstand a lot of heat – '

He broke off as Biggles waved him to silence. Everyone tensed, listening hard, and heard the roar of engines echoing through the deserted streets. Swiftly, the party scurried to take cover in the surrounding buildings – and not a moment too soon, as two heavy German transporters draped with camouflage netting entered the square on the far side, disgorging about twenty soldiers clad in drab-looking grey fatigues. Working in teams, they erected a line of wooden posts along the side wall of the town hall. When this was completed they returned to the wagons, donned ear-protectors and heavy silver gauntlets that came up to their elbows, before hauling out several humped shapes and carrying them over their shoulders like brown sacks of flour.

'Look!' Ginger gave a hoarse cry of outrage. 'They're tying some of our chaps to those stakes!'

Algy half-rose in alarm behind the crumbling wall, his service revolver gripped tightly in his gloved fist. 'We've got to save them!'

'Not so fast,' rapped out Biggles tersely, peering with hawklike intensity across the square. 'Look.'

Two of the soldiers were propping up a British

114

Tommy, who judging from his manner was either drunk or already dead. His head in the tin helmet drooped and his arms dangled down to his knees. As the Germans fastened the ropes, pulling him upright, his face came into view. It was white, with rudimentary features, and made of plaster.

'They're just . . . dummies,' gasped Ginger, thunderstruck.

Biggles nodded pensively, and gnawed his lower lip. 'They must be getting ready to aim the weapon.' A hard look came into his eyes. 'It must be near here somewhere . . .'

Jim edged along under cover of the wall and crouched next to Biggles. He pointed beyond the German transporters to where a British Army artillery piece and a British tank were being manoeuvred into position between two of the white domelike structures by another work team in their peculiar protective gear.

'Look – more of those igloos.'

It seemed to Biggles that this was some kind of target area, with dummy troops and captured British artillery bang in the centre of the bull's-eye. That might also explain the devastation of the town and the total absence of any civilian population. He was mulling over these thoughts when the wail of a klaxon blared out across the square.

The effect was dramatic and instantaneous.

The men tying up the dummies hurriedly finished their task and ran for the white domes, quickly followed by the team that had been positioning the field piece and tank. It almost looked like panic-stations as they piled inside, jostling and shoving.

Jim grabbed Biggles by the arm. 'What's that horn mean?' he asked worriedly.

'That we shouldn't be here,' grated Biggles through his teeth, already on his feet and clambering over the wall.

'Those guys seem to be saying run – don't walk – to the nearest igloo,' Jim panted, helping Debbie over the wall.

'Excellent advice,' agreed Biggles crisply. 'Come on!'

And with that he led the way, skipping over the rubble, towards the white dome on their side of the square, while the klaxon blared out its ominous warning wail.

11

A CLOSE CALL

The door weighed a ton. It took the combined strength of Biggles and Algy to budge it, but finally it swung outwards on greased hinges, a solid foot thick, with a porthole of green-tinted glass almost as deep.

'Ladies first,' muttered Biggles, stretching out a helping hand to Debbie. 'Not much room in there, but I think we'll all squeeze in – '

His jaw sagged in surprise. Debbie caught her breath, standing with one foot poised, as the muzzle of a sub-machine-gun pointed at her stomach, held in the steady, unwavering grip of a heavy-set German corporal with tiny squinting eyes. Jabbing the gun at her, he clambered out, to be followed by three soldiers, one of them also carrying a sub-machine-gun, the other two with rifles.

Biggles glanced warningly at the others, gritting his teeth in frustration. Under normal circumstances they would have made a scrap of it, taken them on without a moment's hesitation, but the automatic weapon was aimed straight at Debbie, the corporal's finger curled round the trigger.

With a weary shrug of resignation, Biggles slowly

raised his arms, Bertie, Algy and Ginger following his lead.

After a slight hesitation, Jim raised his arms also, though he was fuming inside. 'Listen, she can fight,' he told Biggles angrily from the corner of his mouth.

But it was too late. With shouts of *"Raus! Los! Schnell!"* the soldiers jerked their weapons to indicate that the group should stand clear of the dome. The corporal roughly pushed Debbie away from the open hatch, and reached inside to a telephone receiver on a metal cradle. He turned a crank and spoke rapidly into the instrument, his little beady eyes never leaving them.

Biggles lifted his head alertly. His German was far from perfect, but he could have sworn he'd caught the name 'von Stalhein' in the corporal's staccato gabble. After listening raptly for a moment or two, the corporal stiffened.

'Jawohl, Hauptmann!' He slammed the receiver down.

Scrambling through the door, he barked a command, and at once the soldiers started herding the group across the square. Jim had a vague foreboding of what was in store. Biggles knew it for a certainty. It was left to Bertie to voice their fears:

'They're going to use us in place of the dummies!'

'Ruhe!' yelled one of the soldiers, using his rifle butt to silence Bertie, who glared at him ferociously through his monocle.

Debbie confronted the corporal, points of colour burning in her cheeks. 'Listen, I'm an American citizen!' she stormed at him. 'You have no right to treat me this way!'

The beady-eyed corporal scowled and pushed her aside with a derisive sweep of his arm.

'Doesn't anybody here speak English?' demanded Debbie hotly. 'Somebody call the American consulate. Look, two of us here are United States Citizens!' She unzipped her shoulder bag and delved inside. 'I can prove it. I have my passport somewhere in here . . .'

She pulled out a leather pocket-book and flipped it open under the corporal's bulbous nose.

'My passport – my driver's licence – my Diner's Club card – '

With a contemptuous sneer, the corporal slapped the pocket-book out of her hand, and gave her a vicious dig in the small of the back with the snub-nosed muzzle of his gun.

Debbie spun round to face him, her eyes blazing.

'In that case,' she spat, reaching inside her bag, 'I also have my *mace*!'

Debbie whipped out the anti-mugger aerosol and gave the corporal a burst of the stinging spray right in his tiny squinting eyes. He dropped his gun and staggered back with a howl of pain, clawing at his face. Before the guards had time to react, Debbie managed to give the other soldier with the sub-machine-gun a powerful squirt, who cried out and loosed off a full clip, firing blindly in all directions.

Taking advantage of the situation, Biggles pivoted on his heel and swung a fist at one of the guards, catching him on the point of the jaw and sending him spinning to the ground. Jim and the others were soon in the thick of the fray. For several moments the air was filled with thuds, shouts and groans in a free-for-all stand-up brawl.

The blare of the klaxon died away and a low, sinister sound insinuated itself, vibrating the molecules of the air in a maddening frenzy. As if acting on a signal, the Germans broke off the fight and, without even bothering to retreive their weapons, raced as one man for the empty dome, panic in their wild rolling eyes, terror smeared across their faces.

'Quick!' Biggles waved his arm frantically. 'Get to the igloo!'

Algy was the first off the mark, loping along after the Germans, who had a head-start. Close behind him came Ginger, with the somewhat rotund figure of Bertie huffing and puffing in the rear. Biggles and Jim each grabbed one of Debbie's arms and carried her along at the run.

Catching up with the trailing German, Algy stuck out a foot and neatly tripped him. Ginger leapt over the sprawling soldier, who was just about to climb to his feet when Bertie stepped on his head. By now the corporal had reached the dome and leapt inside, his two comrades struggling to follow him but getting jammed in the doorway.

One of them was suddenly grabbed from behind by Algy's long arms and pulled backwards, the momentum sending them both rolling over and over in a tangled heap. Ginger got a grip on the other one and dragged him bodily away, which conveniently allowed the corporal, heedless of his comrades, to start closing the door.

Bertie arrived in the nick of time and grabbed desperately for the door handle. For a second it was touch and go as he strained with all his might to prevent the door closing.

Then Ginger came to his rescue. Having dealt with the other fellow, he sprang to Bertie's aid, and together they yanked the door open, reached inside, and grabbed the corporal by the scruff of the neck and hauled him outside, kicking and screaming and clawing futilely at the door-frame.

Having disposed of him with a boot up the backside, Bertie dusted off his hands and gallantly gestured for Ginger to enter. Being the youngest of the team, Ginger demurred, and politely indicated that Bertie should go first. Bertie accepted. He put one foot inside the dome, and a pair of arms encircled his waist and sent him crashing backwards on top of his adversary. Then the man tripped by Algy arrived, and Ginger too found his hands full, the pair of them locked together as they waltzed away, swapping punches.

Biggles and Jim, supporting Debbie between them, zig-zagged past these three individual battles and lifted the girl through the doorway. Jerking his thumb, Biggles ordered curtly, 'Better join her, laddie,' and while Jim dived inside, turned back to assist the others.

The deep humming vibration had now reached the threshold of human endurance. Its throbbing resonance seemed to penetrate all matter, jarring the skull and making the senses flicker and shimmer unsteadily.

Biggles knew they had seconds at the most to escape its full deadly effect.

Leaping forward, he was just in time to save Ginger having his head smashed in by a brick. Biggles pinioned the attacker's arms and threw him bodily several yards, heaved his young protégé to his feet and pushed him towards the open door.

Algy and Bertie had given a good account of themselves, and they too were running for the dome. They ducked inside, quickly followed by Ginger, with Biggles stepping backwards through the rubble, fists raised, ready to ward off any final assault.

Space inside the dome was cramped, and became even more so as Biggles crawled in. Driven berserk by the high-pitched humming, the Germans attempted one last maddened attack, but were met with a flurry of fists which sent them reeling backwards, giving Biggles the few precious seconds he needed to slam the door shut and ram home the locking levers.

Except for their own harsh breathing, nothing could be heard inside the dome, despite the Germans' frantic pounding on the smooth tiled surface and their gaping, screaming mouths at the portholes. Biggles watched dispassionately as the corporal's hands clawed at the thick green-tinted glass. Then the man's face contorted in agony, and he clamped both grimy hands over his ears, twisting his body as the humming, totally inaudible to those inside the dome, built up to its peak.

Debbie hid her face in Jim's shoulder, not bearing to look any more. It was a truly horrific sight. Wisps of steam started to rise from the corporal's uniform. With body taut, head thrown back, he stumbled away like a drunken man and sprawled full-length in an ice-flecked puddle. The water in the puddle began to boil. Steam rose up around his body. His flesh seemed to be melting into the water.

Ashen-faced, Biggles was staring through the

porthole, his lips compressed into a hard, thin line.

'My God,' he murmured numbly. 'They've done it. They've perfected the bloody sound weapon!'

Jim was having trouble accepting the evidence of his own eyes. Across the square the British artillery piece was glowing white-hot. The tank was surrounded by a pulsating molten glow. Even as he watched, the wall of a house collapsed soundlessly in a swirling blanket of dust, and what few windows remained exploded silently in arcs of glittering fragments.

Colonel Raymond's fear had been fully justified, Jim realised. With such a weapon the Germans could alter the entire course of World War I – rewriting history from that point onwards. And where would that leave Debbie and himself? Trapped at the wrong end of the hole in time?

A buzzer rasped loudly inside the dome, making them all jump. A red warning light near the door went out and a green bulb lit up: the ALL CLEAR signal.

Biggles released the locking levers and tentatively opened the door a crack. All was quiet. He pushed the door open and climbed out slowly, eyes and ears alert. A thin dust was slowly sifting through the air and settling over everything. Nothing moved.

At his gesture, the others started to emerge, looking around curiously. Biggles knelt to examine the body of the corporal, lying in a pool of steaming water. The man appeared to be dead, though there were no visible signs of injury. Biggles lifted the man's arm to check for a pulse and the arm came away in his hands, broken clean off at the shoulder. Biggles dropped the arm with alacrity, feeling the hairs stand up on the back of his neck.

Jim had wandered across to the artillery piece he had seen glowing white-hot, but which now looked perfectly normal. He put his hand close to it, testing for heat, and not feeling anything, touched the steel barrel with his fingertips. He stepped back in alarm as the barrel split apart like a rotten husk and crumbled before his astonished eyes into pulverised dust.

The three other Germans were lying in various frozen postures amongst the debris. Debbie, her curiosity overcoming her fear, approached one of them and gazed down at the man's peaceful face, covered in a layer of fine grey dust. Strange, she thought, there wasn't a mark on him. She reached down slowly and touched his face. Her fingers didn't stop but sank straight through into a soft glutinous pulp. With a strangled cry of revulsion, Debbie whipped her hand away, and part of the corpse's face came with it, sticking to her fingers like soft melted toffee. In the centre was a human eyeball, staring up at her.

Debbie shuddered with revulsion and shook the sticky mess from her fingers. She wanted to scream, but no sound came out of her uselessly working mouth. Cold sweat bathed her forehead. She felt faint and sick to her stomach.

Jim ran to her and held her up, his arms wrapped round her trembling body. It took several moments for the wave of nausea to pass and a faint flush of colour to seep back into her cheeks.

Biggles strode over and called them all together. His face was grey, and his nostrils flared; his grey eyes were as cold and bleak as burnished steel.

'We've seen enough,' he snapped harshly. In the eerie stillness and quiet, his voice cut through the air like a whiplash. 'Let's get back.'

He started off across the square with a grim, resolute step, shoulders hunched, heading for the ruined buildings.

* * *

As they moved from the street into the empty shell of the house where the entrance to the tunnel was located, Biggles suddenly lifted a cautioning hand, bringing the party to a halt. He motioned to Algy, Bertie and Ginger to take up positions, touching a finger to his lips to indicate silence, and then crept stealthily forward, sub-machine-gun at the ready.

Stepping on tip-toe through the rubble, Biggles circled the shaft, pausing now and then to listen. He nodded to himself; his acute hearing hadn't played him false. There was somebody down there in the tunnel.

At that moment a German soldier, wearing one of the hideous elephant-like gas masks, stuck his head up out of the shaft, and ducked back at once. Biggles' face tightened with frustration; this was damned annoying – the tunnel was probably crawling with enemy 'Badgers', as the German underground troops were known. Getting back to their own lines – and with a woman in tow – was going to be impossible until they'd been flushed out.

Beckoning his comrades forward with a jerk of his head, he stepped up to the ladder and fired a burst into the shaft. There was a tremendous clatter of small arms fire from below and bullets zinged everywhere, ripping holes out of the bare plaster and whining off into space through the open roof. Biggles went down on one knee, the others standing at his shoulder, and together they poured a hail of lead into the shaft, temporarily silencing the opposition.

Biggles squinted at Jim through the swirling cordite fumes.

'You two stay up here until we get them cleaned out,' he ordered, slipping the strap from his shoulder and tossing the sub-machine-gun to Jim, who caught it gingerly.

Biggles unclipped a splinter grenade from his belt, pulled the pin and tossed it into the shaft. Smoke and flame erupted from the hole. Before it had cleared, Biggles had donned his gas mask, drawn his service revolver, and leapt down the ladder under covering fire from his comrades. No sooner had he vanished than they scrambled quickly after him, pulling on their gas masks.

The sound of firing had alerted troops elsewhere in the small town, who now came running through the littered streets and shattered buildings. Standing at an open window, Debbie spotted them and alerted Jim with a cry.

The next moment she was swept from view as Jim dragged her to the floor – not an instant too soon as shots raked the window-frame, showering them in splinters. Telling her to lie flat, he crawled to the doorway and peered out. A dozen or so grey figures were dodging along the street, orange flame stabbing from their rifles and automatic weapons.

Jim got to his feet, glancing desperately over his

shoulder to the shaft, in which, from the sound of it, another fierce battle was raging. Trapped between hell and high water. He gritted his teeth, hoisted the heavy, unfamiliar weapon, and, murmuring a quick fervent prayer, sprayed an arc of fire into the street.

Thirty feet below, Biggles had made it as far as the narrow spur linking the shaft to the main tunnel. Already two of the enemy lay dead behind him. Now to flush out the rest. He had one grenade left. Tossing it into the darkness, he crouched against the slimy wall, arms shielding his head, and felt the scorching blast slam against him, like an exploding furnace. Any poor devil caught in that wouldn't stand an earthly.

The explosion had done more damage than Biggles hoped or expected. The shock-wave had buffeted along the tunnel, bringing down part of the roof and nearly burying Ginger under several tons of rock and broken bricks. Algy and Bertie were pulling him free as Biggles crawled back, switching on the lantern and peering at them through the choking dust.

'It's clear. We can go ahead,' he reported, wiping his mouth with his scarf.

'Too late,' growled Bertie, shaking his head sombrely. 'The bally shaft's caved in.'

Biggles stared with dismay at the rockfall completely blocking the shaft. It would take a platoon of sappers a month of Sundays to clear that little lot.

In the ruined house above, Jim turned away from the smoking heap of rubble where the shaft had once been, his expression fraught with concern.

'I hope Biggles made it,' he muttered worriedly.

'Biggles!' yelled Debbie, outraged. 'What about us?'

She had a point, Jim conceded, swinging back to face the onslaught from the street. He crouched underneath the window, checking the magazine, with Debbie clinging to his arm. There couldn't be more than a dozen rounds left in the clip. Enough for one final burst. Okay, if that's the way it had to be . . .

Jim curled his finger round the trigger. He'd go out with a bang and not a whimper. He jumped up, in full view of the advancing troops. Framed in the window, he blasted away for all he was worth, unaware of the softly shimmering yellow glow surrounding him.

12

MANHUNT

It would have been difficult to say who was the more surprised – Jim or the occupants of the police car, including Chuck, who dived to the floor as a hail of machine-gun bullets punched holes in the doors and shattered the windows with a resounding crash.

Jim stood rooted to the spot, the smoking gun in his hands, gazing with open-mouthed horror at the bullet-riddled car on the Northern Approach to Tower Bridge. To the police it must have seemed that he and Debbie had vanished one second, only to reappear the next – instantly transformed into a pair of grimy, smoke-blackened and bedraggled desperados toting a deadly weapon that had nearly wiped out a carload of the London Metropolitan Force, 'D' Division, and an overweight American tourist.

One thing for certain, Jim realised. This was no time for excuses, apologies or explanations. He could spend the rest of his life in chains in the Tower of London and still they wouldn't believe him.

Grabbing Debbie by the hand, he pulled her down a flight of stone steps which connected the Northern Approach road to the maze of warehouses and wharves that comprised the old dockland area of St Katharine's Dock, long since fallen into disuse. Tall buildings of corroding brick loomed all around them, dissected by narrow dingy alleyways which Jim followed blindly, hoping against hope that they wouldn't lead him into a dead end or to the water's edge.

His hope wasn't fulfilled. With footsteps pounding behind them, Jim and Debbie turned a corner to find themselves faced by a blank brick wall. There wasn't even a door or a window. Jim pulled her into the thin shadow of the building, his eyes frantically searching for an escape route.

'You understand now,' Jim gasped, his chest heaving. 'I've got to get to Colonel Raymond!'

Debbie could only nod breathlessly. She understood only too well. Her eyes widened and she gave Jim a shove. Bolted to the wall of the building opposite, a rusty iron ladder led up to the roof. Jim gave her hand a final squeeze, slung the weapon over his shoulder and started climbing, three rungs at a time.

Minutes later the police arrived in the alley to find a very distressed young woman, her hair awry and her clothing torn, slumped against the wall. Debbie turned a pitiful tear-stained face to them, the picture of ravaged womanhood.

'You okay, Miss?' demanded the young officer grimly, noting her condition.

'I – I think so,' Debbie stammered. She gave a tiny terrified whimper. 'The beast . . . he went that way.'

She pointed farther along the alley, back the way they had come, and as they ran off allowed herself a little secret smile. Only a small victory, but perhaps a crucial one.

* * *

Although for the moment Jim had shaken off the
police, he was under no illusion that he would remain
undetected for long. Somebody splattering a police
car on the streets of London with a sub-machine-gun
would very soon experience the reach, and the
weight, of the long arm of the British law. Jim was
right – and sooner than he expected.

By keeping to the rooftops he had hoped to evade
his pursuers down on the ground, but he hadn't
reckoned on the threat from up above.

Climbing a steeply tiled roof, not even daring to
think of the dizzying three hundred foot drop beyond
the edge of the flimsy guttering, Jim's heart leapt into
his mouth as a sleek black helicopter with twin
weapons' pods suddenly loomed up from the side of
the building, almost causing him to lose his grip.

A Bell JetRanger specially modified for anti-
terrorist duties, with armour-plating and an uprated
turboshaft engine, its formidable armament included
two 7.62mm cannons and a nest of laser-guided rock-
ets.

For a frozen instant of eternity Jim was outlined
there, on the apex of the roof, a sitting target for the
police marksman with the telescopic rifle leaning out
of the rear bay, swinging round in his harness as the
helicopter circled and swooped nearer. The whirling
blades of the machine beat the air in solid thudding
waves, almost dislodging Jim from his precarious
perch.

'STOP OR WE'LL SHOOT!'

A voice like rolling thunder boomed from two huge
ball-shaped speakers mounted on either side of the
helicopter's black streamlined body.

Jim didn't hesitate, but leapt, feet-first, arms spread wide, and slid on his backside down the sloping tiles, hit the guttering, and jumped across a yawning gap to land on a flat concrete roof. He scrambled up and sprinted for the only protection on offer – a low brick structure twenty yards away across the exposed roof.

The shadow of the helicopter blocked out the weak winter sun as it made a tight banking turn and came in low, the marksman picking up the running figure in the cross-hairs of his sights.

'STOP!'

It was the voice of thunder's final warning.

Jim was just a few despairing feet away from the brick structure when the marksman fired, and Jim felt himself grasped as if by a powerful hand and slammed against the crumbling brickwork, the breath knocked from his lungs. The powerful hand that *had* yanked him under cover released its hold, and Jim could only gape and squeak with his last gasp of breath, 'What the – '

'Keep still!'

Jim sucked in air and found his voice. 'How did you get here?'

'I've no idea,' confessed Biggles, somewhat ruefully, his strong thoughtful face, framed in leather helmet and goggles, wearing an expression of frank bewilderment.

Jim understood, or thought he did. 'You've fallen through the hole in time . . . the same thing that happened to me!'

Biggles eyed him narrowly, but chose not to respond. Instead he jerked his gloved thumb skyward. 'What do you call that?' he asked tersely.

'That . . . it's a helicopter. They're trying to kill me,' Jim said, suddenly remembering the predicament he was in, and added shortly, 'You too now, probably.'

Biggles nodded. Being shot at was nothing new for a World War I air ace. 'Where are you trying to get to?'

'Tower Bridge. You know it?'

'Of course.' Biggles unbuckled a flap and withdrew his Very Pistol, a short-barrelled large-bore pistol used for firing signal flares. He slammed a fat red cartridge into the breech and cocked the hammer. 'Get ready to run.'

The airman went down on one knee, steadying his aim with his left arm and sighting along his right, and waited with cool nerves for the helicopter to come within range. As it turned and came at them head-on, looking like a menacing black shark cruising in for the kill, Biggles fired. There was a short fizzing orange streak which ended in an intensely brilliant ball of light, throwing out phosphorescent streamers, as the flare exploded directly above the curved tinted canopy.

Startled and half-blinded, the pilot veered sharply away, giving Biggles and Jim the opportunity they needed.

Racing at full pelt across the flat roof, they leapt over a low concrete parapet and ducked into the narrow space between the wall and a wooden signboard, emblazoned with the faded, peeling name of a shipping line of a bygone age, which overlooked the broad grey curve of the Thames.

From here they could see Tower Bridge, across the

deserted wharves and derelict warehouses of the old dockland. The problem was getting there.

For Jim, the next fifteen minutes had the white-knuckled, gut-churning quality of his least favourite nightmare as he followed Biggles up, down and over the jumble of rooftops, teetering along precipitous ledges with vertical drops yawning below that made his head spin. Once or twice they caught glimpses of blue-uniformed figures on the ground, scurrying like ants through the alleyways. A cordon of police vehicles, their lights flashing, had sealed off the Northern Approach to the bridge, Jim saw, as he and Biggles clambered to the crown of a slate roof and skidded down the other side. Biggles glanced over his shoulder, a mischievous twinkle in his eyes, and nodded to a wooden ladder poking up above the guttering. The very thing, placed there by Providence – which turned out to be a builder's labourer, whose astonished face peered out of an upper window as Biggles whizzed past him with a cheery 'Mind if I borrow your ladder, sir?'

Once on terra firma, they moved cautiously through the alleyways, dodging round corners and keeping close to the tall shuttered buildings. With his unerring sense of direction, Biggles had brought them to within a stone's throw of the granite base of the northern tower of the bridge.

But this, the final leg, was doubtless going to prove the most hazardous of all – the entire area cordoned off with police roadblocks and swarming with armed special combat squads.

A smoky fire was burning on a piece of waste ground. Lounging around it a bored-looking group of young people twitched their bodies and bobbed their heads to the raw throbbing beat of a punk band, bellowing incomprehensible words at full volume from the large stereo speakers of a portable tape-machine.

Of all the sights that might have astounded Biggles in modern London, this was surely the most bizarre. Spiky plumed heads dyed day-glo pink reared up above black-rimmed eyes radiating streaks of purple and primrose yellow. Chains and bangles dangled from ear-lobes, safety-pins were skewered through nostrils. Padlocks, dog-leads and copper piping hung from silver-studded leather belts. Through ragged gaps in their torn T-shirts and jeans, elaborate tattoos adorned the limbs of both sexes in a riotous rainbow of colour.

A stupefied glaze had come over Biggles' eyes as he tried to take in this spectacle. 'Great Scott,' he breathed incredulously, at last. 'It's beyond comprehension . . .'

Jim nodded, in complete agreement. 'What *happened* to you?' he asked, voicing the question that had been nagging at him ever since the airman made his dramatic appearance.

Biggles shook his head slowly and said with a frown, 'I was in my plane . . . the Huns had overrun our front lines, and I went up to try and locate the weapon.'

He shrugged, clearly at a loss.

'In Tower Bridge,' said Jim, nodding in that direction, 'is the guy who has your aerial photographs.'

Some of the punk rockers were drifting off along the street. As one of them passed by he nudged his companion, a girl with a single tuft of green hair sprouting out of a shaven head and a brass ring through her nose, and they both cast appreciative glances at Biggles' First World War flying gear.

This gave Biggles an idea. Taking Jim by the arm, he pulled him into the straggling procession, winding its way along the street and up the steps past the ring of police on the main road.

For a second Jim thought Biggles had gone crazy. Then he cottoned on. He yanked up his collar and swathed his face with his scarf, while Biggles hunched deeper into his fur-lined flying jacket and pulled down his goggles. Keeping in the midst of the punk rockers, and to the earth-shattering blast from the stereo speakers, they shambled by under the noses of the police, who didn't even spare them a disinterested glance.

Twenty yards farther on along the bridge, and safely past the cordon, Jim tapped Biggles on the arm. There it was.

Together they sidled to the edge of the procession and calmly stepped across the pavement, vanishing in a trice through the iron-bound door of No. 1–A.

*   *   *

Jim climbed the stairs and pushed open the door, standing to one side. Biggles strode past him into the sepulchral quiet of the panelled room, with its books and framed prints and stained-glass windows, tugging off his flying helmet and goggles and looking round with a mildly puzzled air.

Colonel Raymond laid down his magnifying glass and the photograph he had been perusing. Very slowly he rose from his armchair, a slight tremor of shocked recognition passing swiftly over his face. He moved forward into the light, a strange radiance of joyful expectancy filling his eyes.

'. . . *Biggles*!'

Biggles blinked, and cocked his head to one side.

'Have I met you, sir?' he asked hesitantly.

The colonel's lower lip quivered.

'I'm William Raymond.'

There was absolute silence during which Biggles stared at the slender, erect form before him in total amazement. Then he said softly, 'Captain Raymond. Good God.'

With tears misting his eyes, the colonel awkwardly wrapped his arms around the young airman and hugged him. 'How I've missed you, old friend,' he murmured huskily.

'I'm sorry, I – I didn't recognise you,' confessed Biggles, drawing back to look intently into the faded blue eyes, noting the lined features and hollow cheeks.

'Yes – ' Raymond cleared his throat and admitted with a faint wry smile, 'the years have taken their toll.'

Biggles' eye fell on a framed photograph, which he took down and gazed at in quiet wonder. A group of four young men in flying kit standing in front of the single-bladed wooden propeller of a Sopwith Camel.

'It's the four of us,' murmured Biggles, fascinated. 'Bertie, Algy, Ginger . . . and me.'

'Exactly.' Raymond tapped the glass with his finger. 'It was taken when our squadron, No. 266, RFC, received its first commendation.' He glanced up with a warm smile. 'I was very proud of all of you.'

'That was only last month,' exclaimed Biggles, half to himself. 'Extraordinary . . .'

'Tell me,' inquired the colonel curiously. 'How did you get here?'

'Damned if I know,' muttered Biggles, with a shake of his head, and raised a perplexed eyebrow at Jim.

'I was about to be shot and Biggles materialised and saved my life,' Jim explained.

'I would never have believed it if I hadn't experienced it,' admitted Biggles, still quite bewildered by the whole episode.

Colonel Raymond stroked his chin pensively. 'So . . . apparently the hole in time goes both ways,' he conjectured. 'It opens when one or the other of you is in mortal danger.'

Nodding to himself, he led them to the table, taking up the large glossy print and magnifying glass.

'Here is the photograph you need – I developed the plate that Ferguson left with me. The weapon is well camouflaged but I've used computer enhancement to show it in more detail.'

'Computer . . . enhancement?' asked Biggles haltingly, with a puzzled frown.

Colonel Raymond patted his shoulder. 'Never mind, old friend,' he smiled, handing Biggles the photograph and magnifying glass. 'I've marked the weapon's position for you.'

After studying the print with rapt concentration for a while, Biggles looked up, his jaw tightening. He slipped the photograph into his pocket and pulled on his helmet.

'Right,' he announced briskly. 'Time we were off.'

'There's police everywhere,' said Jim anxiously, peering through the narrow leaded window. 'Any idea how we get out of here?'

138

Biggles glanced round, his keen eyes raking the room. His mouth gave a humorous twitch as he strode over to the corner where the equipment from Colonel Raymond's mountaineering days was kept. Shouldering a heavy coil of rope, he tossed another coil to Jim, and looked meaningfully at the colonel.

A ghost of a smile flitted across Raymond's face. Leading them through to an adjoining room whose windows overlooked the central span of the bridge, he pointed with a thin, veined hand.

'Go along there, across the bridge, and down the other side.' His brows knitted in a frown as he turned to face them. 'How will you get back . . . to the past?' asked the colonel worriedly.

'I'll find a way.'

Colonel Raymond smiled. He had complete faith and confidence in his old friend. If any man alive could do it, Biggles was that man.

Swallowing a painful lump in his throat, the colonel gripped the arms of the two young men in a strong, warm clasp.

'Godspeed – to both of you!'

Biggles looked deeply into the faded blue eyes for the last time; between the two was a bond of respect and comradeship that time couldn't dim. He unlatched the window and swung himself up on to the stone sill. Two hundred and fifty feet below, the river swirled muddily round the massive granite blocks of the tower.

Jim blanched when he saw the drop.

'Do what I do,' ordered Biggles curtly.

'Yeah,' Jim croaked. That's precisely what he was afraid of. 'But what are you gonna do?' he asked tremulously.

13

RETURN TO THE PAST

Jim had found himself in some hairy situations since becoming embroiled in this mad adventure, but this one took the prize up to now, he reflected gloomily, watching dry-mouthed as Biggles edged slowly along the central fixed span linking the twin towers of the bridge.

One hand held out for balance, the other clutching the coil of rope on his shoulder, Biggles moved along the narrow iron girder, like a fly balanced precariously on a spider's thread. Jim took a deep breath and climbed out after him, a reluctant and extremely nervous second fly. A chill wind whistled through his quaking legs.

Down on the black ribbon of roadway far below them, tiny dots of people and cars no bigger than matchboxes surged back and forth through the police cordons. All it needed was for just one of those dots to glance upwards, Jim thought, and the game would be over.

They were within a few yards of the further tower when Jim got a shock that almost sent him toppling – for suddenly out of the sky swooped the sleek black shape of the JetRanger. It banked and shimmied down to land near the base of the bridge. Figures in flak jackets, accompanied by the pilot, jumped out and disappeared from view.

Biggles pulled Jim to the relative safety of a ledge. He was looking at the helicopter with a certain thoughtful interest. He came quickly to a decision, tied one end of the rope to the girder, and swiftly and expertly fashioned a seat by looping the rope round his waist.

'I have an idea,' he told Jim, a devilish twinkle lurking in his eyes. And then with a brisk, 'Follow me,' launched himself into space.

With his life depending on it, Jim did his utmost to comply.

Copying everything Biggles did, he secured the rope, made a loop, and not allowing any time for second thoughts, pushed himself off, teeth gritted, body rigid with fear. Down he dropped, the sheer side of the tower rushing past in a pale blur, the rope rasping and whining through his gloved hands like a banshee's wail, its friction burning through the leather until his palms felt to be on fire.

Biggles clapped him on the shoulder as he touched the ground. Judging by the expression on his face, thought Jim moodily, he actually seemed to be enjoying all this.

White scarf flapping behind him, Biggles sprinted away, leapt over a wall and raced across to the helicopter, its rotor blades still gently idling. There was no one inside. His eyes alight with feverish curiosity, Biggles looked the machine over with an airman's appreciation. Almost reverently he traced his hand along the smooth black hull, noting the twin weapons' pods and the thrusting blunt muzzles of the 7.62mm cannons.

'Damn me!' he exclaimed excitedly. 'What an ingenious contraption!'

'What are you doing?' Jim gasped as Biggles slid open the cockpit hatch and clambered into the pilot's seat. Already he was fiddling experimentally with the controls. He looked up with a triumphant grin as the 400hp turboshaft jet power unit whined into life and the 33-foot rotor started to spin.

'*Get out of there before they see us!*' yelled Jim, hopping up and down.

Biggles stuffed his leather flying helmet and goggles into his pocket and donned the pilot's shiny modern version with the tinted visor. He waved to Jim to get in. Jim shook his head vehemently.

'What do you think you're doing?' Jim was forced to shout at the top of his lungs as Biggles pushed the throttle open and the engine responded with a full-blooded surge of power. 'Leave it alone and get out at once!'

Biggles found the rotor pitch control and delicately toyed with it. The JetRanger bumped on the ground a couple of times and began to rise.

'Clever!' he shouted above the screaming whine of the engine. 'The plane can be tilted to create an airscrew effect.'

He fastened his seat harness and grasped the control column.

'Better get in!'

Jim gaped at him.

'You're not seriously intending to fly this thing – you don't know how!'

'If you can fly a Sopwith Camel you can fly any-thing,' Biggles told him cheerfully. 'Get in or stay out.'

Jim had a split-second to make up his mind as the JetRanger lifted into the air. He made it up and jumped, grabbing the lower strut of the landing float and hanging on grimly as Biggles pushed the throttle wide and increased the rotor pitch. The helicopter rose straight up, yawing crazily, and started to spin like a top.

With both arms wrapped round the strut, Jim looked down between his legs at the whirling ground fifty feet below, and shut his eyes tightly. Another nightmare to add to the list.

Biggles wore a frown of annoyance as he glanced over his shoulder. 'Blast, the little propeller at the back ought to compensate!' he muttered to himself.

Bending forward, he tested and tried out the various controls. In addition to the central control column, which he had already decided controlled up and down movement, there was a lever with a moulded rubber grip conveniently placed for his left hand. He eased it forward slightly, and then back. The machine stopped spinning, which was fine, but then started going backwards. Damn! Not as easy as he thought.

Dangling below, Jim opened his eyes. The blood drained from his face.

'You're going to hit the bridge!' he screamed.

Coolly, Biggles steadied the control column with one hand and adjusted the rotor pitch with the other. The JetRanger began to respond to his instinctive touch, achieving a more stable trim. Biggles grunted to himself, 'feeling' the machine now, confident he was getting the hang of it. Slowly ascending, be brought it round in a wide gentle turn, clearing the central span of the bridge between the towers.

On the bridge itself, the pale upturned faces of the chopper pilot and the anti-terrorist squad gazed up in dumbfounded amazement as the helicopter and its dangling passenger headed downriver.

'Try and get in,' Biggles called out to Jim, who after a bit of a struggle hauled himself up and crawled into the cockpit and slumped back in the co-pilot's seat.

'Don't ever do that again,' he mumbled weakly, white-faced and trembling.

Biggles gestured that he couldn't hear above the engine's high-pitched whine and the thudding *whoosh whoosh whoosh* of the whirling blades. He pointed to a helmet. Jim put it on, and the airman's breezy greeting sounded in his ear over the intercom.

'Welcome on board!'

Jim scowled at him. After they made this guy they broke the mould. And probably just as well. He quickly buckled himself into his harness and looked across in some alarm as the helicopter dipped and rose again, yawed sickeningly to left and right. But it was only Biggles, testing out the machine's capability, half-smiling to himself in rapt concentration.

Biggles spoke into the button mike attached to his helmet:

'It's more difficult than I thought . . .'

'Why don't you try this?' Jim reached out and, before Biggles could reply, jabbed a large red button marked AUTOPILOT.

At once the JetRanger's streamlined nose tilted

steeply downwards and the tail started to spin round and round above their heads as the machine went into an uncontrollable dive.

'Hang on!' shouted Biggles through his teeth. 'We're going down!'

Through the curved canopy, the river loomed towards them with terrifying speed. Jim braced himself for the impact, his stomach turning queasy somersaults. Biggles, face taut and nostrils pinched with strain, pulled back on the column with all his strength, but the helicopter apparently had a will of its own, defying even his attempts to right it.

Plunging down, they were only feet from the grey, slow-moving water when something strange happened. The helicopter was suddenly enveloped in a fierce electrical storm, a million blue fireflies dancing and jittering over every square inch of the tinted canopy and black armoured body and whirling rotors.

And then something stranger still.

One moment the JetRanger, bathed in a flickering blue glow, was falling into the river – the next it had vanished in a puff of carbonised particles, which were borne slowly downstream on the breeze.

* * *

The big push had ground into a wearisome stalemate, both sides bogged down in a sea of churned-up mud, barbed-wire and straggling trenches knee-deep in freezing water.

From a slight rise, sheltered by a few stunted and shattered trees, the British NCO trained his binoculars on the shell-hole about forty yards into no-mans land. A dozen of the enemy had taken cover there and it was his job to dig them out. It was a suicide mission; anyone crossing that open ground in daylight would be mown down before he'd gone ten paces.

Sporadic firing rattled back and forth between the lines, interspersed with the occasional shriek of a mortar. Distantly, the heavy booming rumble of the big guns reverberated over the blasted landscape. Winkling those blighters out was going to be tough, the NCO decided.

He tensed into an attitude of listening. Raising his head warily, he looked carefully all about him. Even from this distance he could see the Germans in the shell-hole swivelling their heads to discover the source of the strange, unearthly sound, like giant wings beating back the air in thudding waves. The NCO had certainly never heard anything like it in his life before.

Gradually the noise of battle died away. An eerie silence fell. Troops on both sides of the line were gazing up at the sky, puzzlement and an uneasy foreboding in their tired, grimy faces.

From out of the murk and drifting smoke, an ominous black shape materialised as if from nowhere.

Racing towards them at zero feet, the JetRanger roared over the silent battlefield, the shrill whine of its 400hp turboshaft engine deafening those below. The men in the trenches clapped their hands over their ears and stood gaping. Some, thinking it to be a secret flying weapon developed by the other side, abandoned their firing positions and dived to the bottom of the deepest trench they could find. The NCO, a devout Catholic, crossed himself and pressed his hands together.

Grinning broadly, Jim slapped Biggles on the shoulder.

'We're back in 1917 – we did it!'

'Colonel Raymond was right,' averred Biggles, watching the battlefield and the blurred blobs of faces zip by beneath them. 'Mutual danger opens the hole in time.'

Checking his position against the British Front Line, Biggles set course for base, the operational airfield of 266 Squadron. A few minutes later he pointed a gloved finger at the cluster of wooden buildings and bell-tents, with the ruined farmhouse behind them. Camels and SE5s and the old dependable Strutter were parked on the tarmac outside the makeshift hangars.

Figures ran out on to the sward and stood in groups, swivelling round and round and gesticulating at the sky as the helicopter made a series of tight banking spirals over the squadron office hut.

The corner of Biggles' mouth twitched in a mischievous crooked grin. He stuck out his hand.

'Give me that gadget . . . that magnifies the voice.'

Jim handed him the microphone and turned up the speaker volume on the instrument panel.

'Let's wake 'em up,' muttered Biggles gleefully, and thumbed the button.

'ALGY! BERTIE! GINGER! ON YOUR FEET!'

Biggles' voice boomed and echoed like the crack of doom over the airfield, literally rocking the pilots and ground crews back on their heels. Biggles laughed delightedly as he recognised Smyth, his fitter-mechanic, turn away from working on a machine, his jaw dropping slackly open. There too was 'Wat'

Tyler, the Recording Officer, emerging from the squadron office at the run, a bundle of papers in his hand.

Then he spied the tall figure of Algy, standing outside the mess hut, hands on hips, staring with incredulous eyes at the bizarre machine with the propeller on top, circling overhead.

'MEET ME ON THE RUNWAY, DOUBLE-QUICK!'

Algy jumped as if jabbed with a pin. He looked five ways at once, and then ran to the 'A' Flight hangar, to be joined by Bertie and Ginger. The trio of flyers shaded their eyes and watched as Biggles hovered gently down and brought the JetRanger to a neat pinpoint landing not ten feet from where they stood.

Biggles unbuckled his straps, slid the hatch open and jumped out, tossing the helmet into the cockpit. He ruffled his hand through his hair, a broad grin plastered from ear to ear. His three comrades-in-arms clustered round him, slapping him on the back and chattering ten-to-the-dozen, while Jim looked on.

'Damn me, it *is* you!' chortled Algy ecstatically. 'I didn't believe my ears . . .'

'We thought that when your plane crashed . . .' Bertie began sombrely, then his expression brightened. He polished his monocle briskly and stuck it back in his eye for a closer inspection of the mysterious machine. 'What's this thing – a flying windmill?' he inquired humorously.

'I'll explain later,' said Biggles crisply. He glanced round, a harder light entering his keen grey eyes. 'Right now I need a dozen Cooper bombs, a Lewis gun, plenty of ammunition – and a bit of luck!'

'We'll guarantee the bombs, gun and ammo, anyway,' Algy promised him eagerly.

Biggles strode purposefully over to the office. 'Ginger, get full battle kits for all of you – machine-guns and grenades.'

Ginger's eyebrows shot up excitedly. 'We going up in your windmill?'

'Afraid not,' retorted Biggles grimly. 'I'm going to use it to attack the sound weapon. You three take your machines to the convent – protect the civilians.' A dark shadow passed across his face. 'The Huns may decide to take reprisals,' he added stonily.

'We'll change their minds for 'em,' growled Bertie, pulling on his leather gauntlets. 'Let's go, lads!'

The three hurried away to get organised. Biggles turned to Jim.

'You still with me, Ferguson?' he asked lightly, a twinkle of devilment in his eyes. 'What say we show that sausage guzzler what this crate can do?'

Jim held up a modern automatic rifle he'd found in the JetRanger's cockpit and tapped it meaningfully.

'I say – let's kick some ass, old boy!' he declared spiritedly.

That's what Biggles wanted to hear. He grinned and gave Jim the 'thumbs-up'. It was time to strike back.

14

BIGGLES STRIKES BACK

The perfect white orb of the winter sun in the icy blue sky flashed its blinding glare on the tinted canopy of the helicopter as it sped low over the reserve trenches of the British positions. For once the grey blanket of cloud had been swept away on a cutting easterly wind, leaving the sky clear and translucent, as if washed clean. Below, the muddy brown pockmarked earth was bathed in unaccustomed brilliant sunshine, like the dusty, cobwebbed corner of a darkened room suddenly exposed to a bright light.

Down there were hundreds of thousands of men, facing each other across barbed-wire entanglements and minefields, waiting for the chance to smash the other side to pieces. The folly of war, reflected Biggles moodily. He was sick and weary of it – the result, he knew, of months of strain and tension at the Front. In all except the most filthy weather, allied airmen were flying an average of 1200 miles a day. The life expectancy of novice pilots, newly arrived from England, was one day.

Biggles grunted, shaking himself out of this black mood. It was irritation born of tiredness. He needed a rest. Maybe after this little party was over he could wangle three days' leave in Paris.

Strapped into the co-pilot's padded seat beside him, Jim sat attentively with the automatic rifle across his knees. At his feet, six 20-pound Cooper hand bombs nestled in the straw bedding of the compartmentalised wooden box.

Peering ahead through the curved canopy, Biggles settled himself a little more squarely in his seat and took a firmer grip on the control column. His authoritative voice came calmly over the headset.

'Better hold on . . . we're crossing the lines.'

From this height, Jim had a grandstand view of the grey-clad German troops crouching in their trenches and dugouts. He could even make out their individual expressions of shocked surprise and mesmerised awe and fear as the JetRanger whirred past overhead, splitting the air with its shrieking jet power unit and thudding blades. One or two of them raised their rifles and took pot shots, though their aim was woefully short as the helicopter streaked past at practically zero altitude.

They were now in dangerous territory, and Biggles kept his eyes peeled, squinting through his fingers for 'the Hun in the sun'.

His vigilance was soon rewarded. A tiny black speck, high up in the wide blue vault of sky, was heading towards them from the east. Biggles smiled with satisfaction. His keen eyes had caught a glint of sun on an aluminium engine cowling.

At once Biggles opened the throttle and altered the rotor pitch, taking the JetRanger up in a zooming climb. The speck, diving towards them, had resolved

itself into a black Fokker Dr-I triplane, the iron
crosses outlined in white on wings and fuselage.

Down it dropped like a stone, the stabbing flashes
of its twin Spandau guns spitting tracers through the
swirling arc of its propeller. Jim lurched back in his
seat as bullets stitched a neat row of holes in the
landing float and grazed the perspex canopy inches
away from his head. He fumbled with the rifle, but
was hopelessly too late as the Fokker swept past in a
wire-screaming dive and whirled round to align itself
on their tail.

Biggles wore a snarling grin through set teeth. He'd
recognised the machine, and the pilot's head inside
the riveted iron mask had confirmed it. His old duelling adversary – Erich von Stalhein. He was going to
enjoy this.

For the moment, however, his mind and his hands
were busily occupied with shaking off their expert and
persistent pursuer.

With a top speed of 150 mph, the JetRanger could
have easily outpaced the Fokker triplane's 85 mph
maximum, but Biggles had other ideas. Throttling
back slightly, he allowed the other machine to close
the distance, and just when he estimated that von
Stalhein was within range, his hand about to slam
down on the gun-levers, Biggles threw the helicopter
into a steep banking turn, the whirling rotor blades at
ninety degrees to the ground.

Try as he might, the pilot of the Fokker couldn't
hold the same line, and had to take some desperate
action to prevent his machine spinning out of control
in a stalling turn.

Jim slid open the hatch and leaned out, the rifle

cradled against his cheek, determined to be ready the next time. Biggles grinned across at him, eyes alight, relishing the dog-fight to the full. As the Fokker turned towards them, he held the helicopter on a level collision course, not deviating by so much as an inch.

'Try this, you sausage guzzler!' he ground out through gritted teeth.

Stabbing flame came from the Fokker's guns as it screamed at them head-on, but the pilot, to his utter amazement, discovered he was firing into thin air as the helicopter abruptly ascended vertically into the sky as if yanked up on a steel wire.

Von Stalhein hauled back the stick and started to chase the rising helicopter, guns blazing. There was a sharp metallic *whang* as a bullet penetrated the steel underbelly, and a fan of tracers streaked past the open hatch on the port side, making Jim hurriedly duck back inside. He scowled at Biggles. That was too damn close for comfort.

'Hang on!' Biggles cried out in warning, and in the next instant the JetRanger plummeted earthwards, blades feathered, while von Stalhein once again found himself firing at empty space.

Screwing his head round, the German pilot searched the sky for the enemy aircraft that had vanished with the baffling abruptness of a magician's trick from the centre of his ring-sight. With a snarl of rage and frustration he spotted it streaking along at ground level, and standing his triplane on its wingtips, dived after it in fresh pursuit.

Biggles glanced over his shoulder as the black Fokker weaved behind them, closing in for the kill. Distantly he heard the stammer of the twin Spandaus.

He peered ahead, a roguish smile flitting across his face. Jinking over the telegraph wires which ran along the side of a railway line, Biggles pointed the helicopter's nose straight between the shining steel tracks. Less than two miles away, a heavily laden munitions train was trundling towards them, its engine belching black smoke. Practically skimming the grass verges on either side of the track, Biggles flew straight at the huge locomotive, the Fokker directly astern and closing rapidly. When it seemed that head-on collision was inevitable, the British flyer casually eased the column back and flipped over the smoke-stack. Von Stalhein blanched as he realised his mistake. Almost too late, he nearly tore the wings off his machine as he wrenched the stick into the pit of his stomach, his undercarriage missing the smoke-stack by a matter of feet.

Looking back over his shoulder, von Stalhein's eyes bulged behind the iron mask with incredulous amazement. Impossible! Even a flyer of Biggles' legendary reputation couldn't have achieved that. Yet there was the train, steaming along as before – and there too was the enemy machine – sitting in the middle of it on a flat bed wagon!

Further attack was clearly out of the question. The train was packed with tons of armaments and high explosives on their way to the Front. A single stray bullet could blow the whole thing sky high.

Raising the revs of the Oberursel engine and lifting the nose to gain altitude, the German air ace slid his flare pistol from its leather pouch. His thin lips curled in a cold smile as he sent a blue and yellow signal flare arcing into the sky leaving a thin trail of smoke spiralling in its wake.

Very well. It was regrettable. But if he couldn't deal with Biggles personally, he knew something that could.

* * *

Watching through the slit in the concrete blockhouse, the Leutnant whipped the binoculars from his eyes, snatched up the telephone, and issued instructions in a flat, guttural bark.

Deep below ground in the reinforced concrete silo, the NCO cradled the receiver and shouted down from the gantry to the ranks of sweating men below, half lost in the drifting wraiths of steam seeping from the cooling vents. Under the supervision of the chief engineer, they bent to their toil, turning the huge cast-iron spoked wheels which released steam pressure to drive the massive turbines and electrical generators.

Behind them at control panels, another rank of men spun valves and operated levers, feeding the generated power through transformers and circuits into the main cable relay. The vast subterranean power hall throbbed with electrical energy and hissed with gusts of steam from the water coolers.

The chief engineer bellowed an order, and the men quickly clamped bulky ear-protectors over their heads.

Then, at a signal from the NCO, he stepped up to the main panel and threw a red stirrup switch. As if from the bowels of the earth, a low vibrating hum slowly built up, shaking the concrete foundations. Gradually it became louder, and louder, and louder still, rising in pitch until the humid steamy air itself seemed to be shrieking in agony.

* * *

Biggles pulled the aerial photograph from his pocket and propped it against the instrument panel. With a sweep of his hand, he indicated the terrain rushing past beneath them.

'This is the area Colonel Raymond marked. Keep your eyes skinned.'

Jim nodded, peering intently through the cockpit canopy. As the helicopter banked to take in a wider vector, he suddenly stiffened against the straps, his face taut with suppressed excitement, and pointed a trembling finger.

'Good God, Biggles – that's it!'

Draped with layers of camouflage netting, a long angular arm topped by a concave silver dish was rising slowly into the air, like a prehistoric reptile rearing up from a primeval swamp.

Jim gawped at it, fascinated and repelled. It had a kind of terrible awesome beauty. The metal arm rose higher until it was fully extended, and the dish started to swivel, a huge baleful eye seeking them out. As it swept in their direction, the low sonic hum swelled to a screeching frenzy, so that the dish and its arm seemed to blur in front of Jim's eyes, the sound setting his teeth on edge with its maddening, high-pitched vibration.

A jerk from Biggles' arm brought him back to his senses. Jim hefted one of the Cooper bombs by its metal handle and braced himself at the open hatch.

The entire machine was being shaken so violently, caught in the full force of the weapon's tremendous power, that he was in danger of being thrown out.

At the controls, Biggles was fighting to keep the JetRanger in the air. Grimacing with the effort, he pushed the column forward, cords of muscle standing out on his neck.

'I'm going in low,' he grated. 'Try to . . . get under the beam.'

As the helicopter swooped nearer to the ground, the silver dish tilted to keep the force-field focused upon it. The sound was horrendous, penetrating Jim's helmet and jarring the bones of his skull. He didn't see how they could ever get near enough to use the hand bombs.

There was a sudden sharp *bang*!. With a fierce splutter of electric sparks, the instrument panel on his side of the cockpit erupted in a blinding flash, thick yellow smoke pouring out and filling the cockpit with its acrid stink.

Jim slid the bomb into its straw nest and grabbed the fire extinguisher, spraying clouds of CO over the fizzing panel and almost blinding Biggles in the process.

Trailing smoke, the helicopter weaved and dodged nearer to the sound weapon, now operating at maximum ultrasonic frequency. As the smoke and fumes cleared from the cockpit, Jim stared through the canopy, his fingers digging into the padded arm-rests. Directly in front of them, filling the sky, the huge silver dish seemed to shimmer as if seen through a heat haze.

White-faced, lips compressed into a thin hard line,

Biggles wrestled with the column, which was almost being torn from his grasp by the juddering vibration.

He shook his head grimly.

'I can't hold her . . . hang on, we're going down . . .'

The streamlined black nose of the JetRanger gave a sickening lurch. The machine began to skid sideways as the rotor blades sought and failed to gain purchase on the air. Glancing about him, Biggles' despairing eye alighted on the microphone on its coiled cable, attached to the panel.

His clipped, decisive tones sounded in Jim's ear.

'Turn that voice box up to full power.'

Jim spun the calibrated dial on the volume control and plucked the microphone from its cradle. 'It's up,' he reported.

'Throw it out.'

'*W–h–a–t*?' Jim stared at the man as if he was mad.

'Do as I say!' snarled Biggles hoarsely.

Jim tossed the microphone through the hatch so that it dangled on the end of its cable, hanging down the side of the machine's curved body. What with the shrill noise keening through his head and the helicopter falling about all over the sky, he thought this to be one final act of insanity born of desperation.

His suspicion was confirmed when Biggles curled his lips back from his teeth in a savage, mirthless grin.

'Chin up, lad!'

What in hell was there to keep his chin up for, Jim wondered numbly. They were beaten. The secret sound weapon had defeated them.

Hovering drunkenly in front of the silver dish, the helicopter was literally being shaken to pieces. Rivets

started to pop. Cracks zig-zagged across the glass dials
on the instrument panel. Everything was a shimmering, shuddering blur, a smear of distorted images
before Jim's dazed vision.

Another shrill note was added to the cacophany of
sound. Jim winced in pain and screwed his eyes shut.
It was as piercing as a dentist's drill hitting a nerve –
the high-pitched squeal of electronic feedback.

Jim blinked his eyes wide open. At last he understood.

'We'll fight sound with sound,' muttered Biggles,
aiming the nose of the JetRanger at the dead-centre of
the dish so that the amplified feedback from the ball
speakers was directed full blast at its source.

'Hang on, old sport – kill or cure!'

In the vast power hall deep underground, the crews
manning the steam turbines, generators and control
panels doubled up in agony, clutching their heads to
shut out the sonic sound-wave they themselves had
created, now beamed back at them magnified a
thousand-fold.

As they ran screaming, the power hall itself began
to tremble violently and disintegrate.

Jagged fissures appeared in the concrete walls. Iron
girders supporting the roof cracked like brittle sticks.
A scalding jet of steam shot thirty feet across the floor
from a ruptured valve. Running out of control, with
no one to operate the safety devices, the pressure in
the turbines built up until the casings cracked apart
like rotten fruit. Gusts of flame and smoke spewed out
of the innards, filling the hall with a scorching blast.

Even though he was prepared for the explosion, the
volcano erupting out of the ground took Biggles by

surprise. The force of it lifted the JetRanger and whirled it skywards like a leaf in a winter's gale. For several minutes it required every ounce of flying skill he possessed to hold the machine on an even trim.

Jim wiped his brow and looked down on the scene of devastation. The countryside was a mass of bright crimson flame and churning oily smoke. He pulled in the microphone and patted it gratefully.

Biggles glanced at him, one eyebrow raised. 'You might say we nuked it, eh?' he mused drily.

Jim blew out his cheeks and nodded.

'Hold tight, I have a promise to keep,' said Biggles crisply, gingerly bringing the helicopter round on a new heading.

As they limped away, a series of explosions, each bigger than the last, rocked the area, culminating in a huge orange fireball streaked with scarlet and purple, billowing upwards, in the centre of it, the single-eyed dish on its long neck tottered and slowly fell into the raging inferno, the metal twisting and buckling like a prehistoric monster in its death throes.

15

THE FINAL ROUND

Crouched on all-fours, Bertie peered through the undergrowth, his monocle winking in the last faint gleams of the setting sun. The soft purple haze of evening lay over the convent, and also a sinister silence, which Bertie most definitely didn't like. If there were any Boche around, they were keeping very quiet about it.

Motioning to the others, he crept forward out of the bushes and pressed himself against the wall surrounding the courtyard, Algy and Ginger taking up positions alongside him. From their expressions he deduced that they didn't much care for the silence either.

Taking care not to let his sub-machine-gun clink against the stone wall, Bertie edged cautiously to the arched entrance and risked a glance into the courtyard. He ducked back at once. A squad of German soldiers, in their drab field-grey uniforms, were lounging against the convent wall having a smoke, their weapons on the ground or propped against the wall. An officer in peaked cap and polished boots was standing, legs braced apart, at the convent door.

Bertie indicated on his fingers the strength of the opposition. Ten, perhaps twelve. Algy nodded. Ginger looked thoughtful.

'Grenade?' Bertie mouthed.

Algy shook his head dubiously. 'Too close to the civilians,' he murmured softly.

'Maybe they'll listen to reason,' whispered Ginger, raising his fair eyebrows at them both.

Algy stared at him, and then looked at Bertie. They shrugged.

The first soldier to notice them blinked. A second caught sight of them and frowned. Gradually a look of total incredulity crept over all their faces, including the officer's. They couldn't believe what they were seeing.

Sauntering casually through the archway into the courtyard, in line abreast, their weapons slung over their shoulders, came the three British flyers, as if out on a pleasant stroll. Their expressions were quite calm and unconcerned. With an easy stride they came to a halt in the centre of the cobbled courtyard and idly surveyed the silent, astonished soldiers.

'I say,' remarked Bertie pleasantly, polishing his monocle on his sleeve. 'Would you chaps consider surrendering?'

The Germans gaped at them for perhaps five seconds, and then as one man made a grab for their rifles.

With smooth, practised precision the flyers swung into action. Algy dropped to one knee, jerking his sub-machine-gun forward, while Bertie and Ginger dived sideways, rolled over, and came up with their weapons levelled, fingers pumping the triggers, flame stabbing from the snub-nosed muzzles. The courtyard boomed and echoed with gunfire and the stutter of automatic weapons. Bullets whined and ricocheted off the cobblestones and sang into the air. The Germans scattered in all directions but couldn't escape the deadly hail of lead from the British flyers.

Algy jumped to his feet, rammed home a fresh clip, and squinted through the swirling blue smoke, the reek of cordite biting the back of his throat. Silence and stillness everywhere. His companions got slowly to their feet, eyes sweeping over the slumped, grey-clad figures for any signs of movement.

A shout from beyond the wall made all three whirl round. Through the stone archway they could see a platoon of German infantrymen running over the open ground, led by an officer brandishing a pistol.

Ginger was first off the mark, closely followed by the others, all three sprinting across the courtyard and bursting through the door into the chapel.

There, in the soft gloom of the fading light filtering through the stained-glass windows, the nuns were crouching protectively over the patients in the narrow trestle beds, and some lying in huddled groups on the flagged floor. The Mother Superior rose from beneath the window, Marie by her side, both with expressions of heartfelt gratitude.

'Stay down, sisters,' warned Algy peremptorily, with a wave of his flattened palm. 'We're not through yet.'

As if to lend weight to his admonition, there was a sporadic clatter of rifle fire, and a tinkle of glass as one of the narrow windows was shattered.

Algy glanced at the others, grim-faced. They

weren't going to be so lucky this time – not with odds of ten to one against.

Undaunted, the three flyers moved to the windows, checking and reloading their weapons. Algy raised his head cautiously above the stone sill. The officer was urging his men forward, some of whom had already infiltrated the courtyard and were dodging about, seeking cover.

It was Ginger, with the keenest hearing, who first heard the thudding throb of the helicopter. He whooped for joy and looked up with shining eyes as it roared over the convent roof and circled the field beyond the wall, settling down with a shrill whine of its turboshaft engine. The German officer looked both ways in panic. His platoon was caught squarely between two lines of fire. Racing back to the archway, he was cut down in a vicious fusillade of automatic fire from the convent windows. Others of his platoon met with the same fate as they made a headlong dash to escape, Biggles and Jim, crouched by the helicopter, picking them off as they scattered blindly across the open field.

In minutes it was all over, the few survivors throwing down their weapons and haring off into the dusk.

The chapel doors were flung open. Algy, Bertie and Ginger emerged into the courtyard, grimy and battle-stained but wreathed in smiles, followed by Marie and the Mother Superior. The slender young dark-haired girl couldn't contain herself. Impatiently, she pushed her way through and ran across the courtyard, her face illuminated with radiant happiness.

Helping Jim to his feet, Biggles turned as Marie burst from the archway and ran to meet him, her hair flowing in the breeze like a dark velvet river. The airman's face, pale and stern, visibly relaxed, the little tired lines round his eyes and mouth slackening as the tension and strain drained from him.

Biggles smiled and strode forward over the grass, his grey eyes softening and losing the steely light of battle. Suddenly he halted. His frame went rigid. His head jerked up. In the same instant he heard Jim's shout of alarm ring out:

'He's back!'

The drone of the black triplane deepened into a menacing throaty growl as it banked steeply and dived towards them, coming in low over the field out of the setting sun.

For an instant Biggles stood frozen to the spot. *Von Stalhein*! he mouthed silently through dry parted lips.

Something clicked in his throat. He threw up his arms mutely, physically trying to ward Marie off, and then the hoarse cry burst raggedly from his lips.

'*Back! For God's sake get back*!'

Marie faltered in her stride and stood limply, exposed on the open field, fear and confusion on her face, not knowing what to do. The black machine came racing in, flashes of light flickering behind the swirling disc of its propeller as the twin Spandaus stuttered their message of death, the tracer bullets kicking up gouts of dirt and stitching two parallel lines down the length of the field. Biggles got to the girl, with Jim a pace behind, and flung her to the ground, feeling the blast of the slipstream as the Fokker roared overhead and zoomed up past the white marble statue of Madonna and Child standing in a little grove of saplings near the convent wall.

Jim raised his head – and almost got it blown off in the shock-wave as the helicopter's fuel tank ignited, a direct hit by a tracer shell. It went up like a torch. Aflame, the rotar blades went spinning into the air like an incandescent Catherine Wheel, bombs and ammunition exploding in a white ball of fire that left nothing behind except a twisted tangle of wreckage, writhing in the fierce heat.

Elated at the destruction he had caused, von Stalhein was performing a victory roll, the dying rays of the sun glinting redly on the aluminium engine cowling.

Biggles scrambled to his feet and glared skywards, an expression of venomous hatred on his face. What wouldn't he have given to be up there right now in his Camel with a pair of fully armed Vickers!

He bent over to help Marie, and his heart stopped. She was lying on her back, head askew, her face deathly pale against the spread of dark hair, one arm flung out on the grass. A black stain was slowly spreading down her left side.

Biggles raised her and gently cradled her head. Marie's eyelids fluttered and she slowly opened her eyes to gaze up at him, a painful smile twisting the corners of her mouth. He bent nearer to catch her faint gasping words.

'I knew . . . you would come for me . . .'

Biggles swallowed hard. 'Marie . . .' he began, but got no further as he saw her dark liquid eyes glaze over and close.

Very calmly, almost mechanically, he lifted the girl up in his arms and carried her to the archway where his comrades and the nuns stood in a silent, stricken group. Algy and Ginger took her from him. Without pausing, he swung round, waving to Jim to join the others, and with even, unhurried strides walked back into the field.

Halting a little distance from the marble statue, Biggles unslung his sub-machine-gun and planted his legs apart. He jerked the bolt and stood awaiting his implacable enemy. His face was drained of all colour, the nostrils pinched and white. In his eyes there was a look of terrible avenging anger.

* * *

The black Fokker triplane made its second run as before, directly out of the sinking blood-red sun, guns blazing.

Racing in almost at ground level, it sprayed two streams of lead at the lone figure standing before the statue, filling the air with the mad clatter of its spitting guns.

Biggles calmly waited for his moment, the sub-machine-gun braced against his hip, knuckles showing white.

Tracer shells gouged the earth all around him, bracketing him in geysers of dirt. A shell splinter struck him over the eye and blood trickled down his cheek. But he did not move; he did not even flinch.

With the triplane looming before him and the shining arc of the airscrew coming straight at him, only then did he open fire. The weapon bucked in his clenched hands like a live thing. But an instant later his face contorted as the trigger went suddenly slack and the weapon jammed. Frantically he worked the bolt, and then with a snarl of rage tossed the gun aside.

Very calmly, Biggles unclipped a grenade from his belt, pulled the pin, and in a cold, controlled fury aimed for the centre of the spinning propeller-boss. Back came his arm, and then swung forward in a blur as he hurled the grenade with every atom of strength he possessed.

Leaning over the side of the cockpit, his icy blue eyes peering through the slits in the iron mask, von Stalhein hurled the dart bomb at the man on the ground. He had the gloating satisfaction of seeing the missile head straight for its target before the Fokker swept past, and over his shoulder glimpsed the vivid flash and gritty grey cloud of the explosion beneath the trailing edge of his lower port wing.

So much for the famous Biggles!

His smile of self-congratulation became fixed and wooden. His feet in their fur-lined boots were uncomfortably hot. Raising his mask from his perspiring face, von Stalhein stared with horror at the flames licking round his ankles, fed by a fractured pipe gushing oil.

On the ground, the thick pall of smoke was drifting slowly away from the ten-foot wide crater. A pale, slender shape appeared through the murk . . . the Madonna and Child, unharmed, gazing serenely into the far distance. The breeze snatched away the last few rags of smoke to reveal another figure, bloody but unbowed, standing in the protective shadow of mother and infant.

Biggles wiped the side of his face with his white silk

scarf and stepped away from the smoking crater, raising his eyes to the black Fokker.

Dispassionately he watched the thin plume of smoke stream from under the cowling, and heard the ragged, hesitant note of the engine as the revolutions died away. The nose dipped. The pilot made a valiant but vain attempt to pull out of the dive as the machine staggered and dropped even more steeply behind a curtain of trees, its engine blazing fiercely.

Turning away, the explosion brightening the sky and ringing in his ears, Biggles walked back across the field with an unutterably weary and defeated tread.

* * *

Algy and Ginger had placed Marie on a bed underneath one of the chapel windows. The Mother Superior knelt beside her, deep in prayer. Jim stood in the shadows, not wishing to intrude into this moment of private grief. Algy and Bertie were looking at the girl with grave, bitter faces. Ginger's eyes were brimming with unshed tears.

Biggles knelt and put his arms round Marie and held her close, his face buried in her dark hair. His shoulders under the worn leather coat moved convulsively. Laying her down tenderly, he gazed upon her face with misty eyes, in which a faint, despairing spark dwindled and died away to nothing.

The Mother Superior made the sign of the cross over the still figure. As she did so, the last light of day broke through the stained-glass window and streamed down, fanning out in a swathe of many colours and forming the image of the Holy Virgin on Marie's pale forehead. Biggles blinked away the moisture from his eyes. He stared and swallowed hard. He didn't believe in miracles – but what else could this possibly be?

A pulse was beating in Marie's slender throat.

She stirred. Her dry lips moved and her eyes opened. She smiled at him.

Biggles smiled back.

He glanced up in gratitude to the light streaming through the window, and something made him turn his head to look at Jim. In the shadows, the young American was surrounded by a shimmering yellow glow. Their eyes met, full of meaning that could not be expressed. Biggles understood. The job that Ferguson had come seventy years into the past to do was over. This particular battle – if not the war – was won. It was the parting of the ways.

With a gesture that was sadly resigned and yet supremely triumphant, the airman raised his hand in a salute of farewell. Presently the glow faded and vanished, and with it so did Jim.

16

TIME AFTER TIME . . .

For Jim, it was the most nerve-racking return of all. Plucked in a trice from the peaceful sanctity of the dim chapel, with the evening sunlight filtering through the stained-glass windows, he suddenly found himself materialising in mid-air, suspended twenty feet above the cold grey waters of the Thames.

The plunge into the icy river shocked the breath from his body. He struggled to the surface, coughing and spluttering, and floundered helplessly until a grappling hook wielded by a burly sergeant hauled him out of the water and dumped him, shivering and teeth chattering, on to the deck of the police launch.

The launch whipped round in a creamy arc and pulled into the quayside of St Katharine's Dock, where he was handed over to the anti-terrorist squad – five tough characters in red berets and flak jackets, armed to the teeth, who bundled him along a wooden gangplank to the dockside and a waiting police van with steel mesh over the windows.

It crossed Jim's mind to wonder if helping to destroy a German secret weapon in the First World War might be some defence against the charge of stealing a three-million-dollar helicopter belonging to the British security services. Gloomily, he rather thought not.

As he was being bustled off the gangplank, a lean, erect figure in a black overcoat stepped forward. With a quiet but unmistakable air of authority, he held out an ID card with an impressive seal.

'Colonel Raymond, Special Air Intelligence. I'll take charge of this man.'

The senior officer, holding Jim by the collar, gaped for a moment at the card, then let go and snapped a smart salute.

Raymond gently took Jim's arm and led him away along the quayside. The grip of his gloved hand tightened as he glanced searchingly into Jim's face.

'Well?' he inquired tersely. 'Did you finish the job?'

Jim paused to wring the cold water of the Thames out of his sweater. He nodded. 'Yes. We finished it.' He shivered and looked curiously into the other man's faded blue eyes.

'Colonel Raymond . . . what happened to Biggles? Did he make it through the war?'

'Oh yes.' The Colonel's voice was quiet but emphatic. 'Biggles and his team continued to serve their country for many years afterwards.'

For a moment the old man gazed into the middle distance, a fond, proud smile playing about his hollow features.

'Is Biggles – still alive?' asked Jim hesitantly.

Raymond blinked and recovered himself. 'Sadly, I don't know. His last mission with the team was to the High Plateau of New Guinea.' He shook his head sombrely. 'No word has so far been received from them.'

'I see.' Jim tightened his lips. Then he gave a shrug. 'I was sort of getting to like him . . .'

'At any rate,' said Colonel Raymond, brightening suddenly, 'you've some consolation – look!'

Jim looked. It was Debbie, waving to him ecstatically from a police car. A moment later she was breathlessly in his arms and kissing him so hard that Jim saw a galaxy of stars swirling madly behind his closed eyelids. There was also, somewhere in there, a gleam of gold, that looked suspiciously to Jim like a wedding ring.

* * *

'Do you, Deborah, take James as your husband?'

The minister gazed down benignly on the radiant young bride in her white lace wedding-gown, and at the tall, elegant young man in grey morning coat and striped trousers, standing before him at the altar.

Behind the happy pair, friends and well-wishers filled the pews of this small parish church, deep in the heart of the English countryside. And there, in the front row, beaming warmly, stood Colonel Raymond, very splendid and dignified in the uniform of Air Commodore from his wartime days, an impressive array of medals and ribbons on his breast.

Debbie glanced up shyly from under her veil and smiled lovingly into Jim's eyes.

'I do,' she murmured softly.

The minister held out his hand. 'The ring, please.'

Jim turned to his best man.

The minister waited, patiently holding out his hand.

And waited . . . his patient Christian smile wearing rather thin as the best man rummaged with chubby hands through the pockets of his tight-fitting morning clothes, his round face getting redder and shinier as he hunted frantically for the ring.

Chuck threw Jim a desperate look of panic and finally came up with a handful of chewing-gum wrappers, toffee papers, crumpled dollar bills, broken pretzels, a plastic fork, and finally, stuck to a blob of melted candy – the ring.

Wiping it on his sleeve, Chuck proudly presented it to Jim, who with a weary sigh accepted the sticky object and turned to Debbie.

Smiling, Jim held the ring up and reached out to take her hand. Debbie jerked back and cried out as a crackling blue spark jumped from his fingertips to hers.

Jim stared at the maze of tiny electric sparks chasing each other over the surface of his hand. He shook his head numbly, a mingled look of horror and despair on his face.

No!

It couldn't be.

Not again.

Not now.

Not –

* * *

Dum–b–dum–dum – dum–b–dum–dum – dum–b–dum–dum –

The throbbing beat of drums and the rhythmic shuffling of naked feet filled the sacrificial cave. On

174

the rough-hewn walls weaved dancing, twisting shadows, thrown by the huge fire blazing in the middle of the sandy floor.

Suddenly the drumbeat ceased.

The circle of tribesmen, daubed from head to foot in white clay, shuffled to a stop and turned their astonished eyes upon the bizarre figure, dressed in morning coat, pearl-grey silk tie and striped trousers, that had magically appeared in their midst. In his hand he held aloft a golden ring that flared brightly in the flickering firelight.

A discordant babble of moans and gibbering cries broke out. The tribesmen backed away and fell to their knees, bowing and praying and hiding their faces from the sight of the divine apparition.

'Quick – untie us!'

Jim spun round at the sound of the familiar voice. His jaw sagged.

Above the blazing fire, partly obscured by smoke, he beheld Biggles, Algy, Bertie and Ginger roped together in a fat-bellied and blackened iron cooking pot. Steam rose around them.

'Well done, man!' gasped Biggles, as Jim leaned over the flames and released their bonds. Throwing off the ropes, the young flyer vaulted out of the pot and clapped Jim on the shoulder.

'Let's get out of here before they stop thinking you're a god and start realising you're an American!'

Leading the way, Biggles sprinted for a dark tunnel, the rest of the team close on his heels.

'In the nick of time, Ferguson,' grinned Biggles, his white scarf fluttering behind him. 'We were in hot water back there.'

'*You* were in hot water? I was about to be married!'

A stone-tipped spear whizzed past Jim's head and buried itself in a wooden carving. Gulping, he glanced up at the quivering shaft.

'Come on!' Biggles rallied them. 'Let's get out of here!'

Deciding that his career as a god was over, Jim needed no second bidding, but dived after the others into the dark mouth of the tunnel, the blood-curdling howl of the pursuing tribesmen ringing in his ears.

As he ran into the darkness, Jim wondered what strange and thrilling new adventures lay ahead. For it seemed clear that Biggles' destiny and his own were inextricably intertwined – not only in the past, but in the present too.

And also in the future.

Time after time . . . you might say.

THE MAKING OF THE FILM

IT WAS inevitable that BIGGLES, idol of millions, survivor of countless adventures and long-term hero of ninety-seven novels by Capt. W. E. Johns, should be brought to the cinema screen as a major British production. But the project took determination worthy of its illustrious character before it could be realised as entertainment to delight the countless brigades of Biggles fans, bring the incredible hero to the attention of a new generation and provide audiences with an exciting hero whose adventures capture the imagination at every twist and turn. In fact, it took a decade for the project to come to fruition.

BIGGLES, the film, is a brand new story created by KENT WALWIN and JOHN GROVES, starring NEIL DICKSON as Biggles, ALEX HYDE WHITE, FIONA HUTCHISON and PETER CUSHING as Colonel Raymond. Biggles' well known pals, Algy, Bertie and Ginger are played by MICHAEL SIBBERY, JAMES SAXON and DANIEL FLYNN. Directed by JOHN HOUGH, the Yellowbill production has ADRIAN SCROPE as executive producer and KENT WALWIN and POM OLIVER as producers. It was filmed on locations in London, extensively around London Bridge, as well as at Stepney and Beckton, in Chislehurst, Kent, Brogborough and Cranfield in Bedfordshire, and at Holdenby House in Northamptonshire. Set both in the early days of Biggles' impressive career as a World War I pilot operating behind enemy lines, and in present-day London, the story captures the

177

elements which made the Biggles books so popular: although he is an absolute and outstanding hero, it is totally possible to relate to his adventures, to identify with them, and to participate in the excitement which constantly surrounds him. In short, Biggles is a *real* hero despite the fact that his roots are in fiction.

In this incredible adventure, Biggles is intent on locating and destroying a secret and deadly weapon which has the potential of changing the outcome of World War I. The screenplay writers have developed a plot which involves a group of young present-day Americans assisting Biggles and his regular team – Algy, Bertie and Ginger – in their deadly quest.

Perhaps it was getting the Biggles story right which made the development of the project so complex. While it was necessary to retain all the characteristics of the hero it was also necessary to give the story ingredients which would make it fully acceptable to present-day audiences.

Kent Walwin, producer and co-writer of the screenplay with John Groves, explains that one of the problems about Biggles which defeated some very good writers who were trying to develop a screenplay, was the prime consideration of whether it would work at the box-office. Trying to make the character come alive from the books often produced a very odd, frozen-in character who didn't ever really come alive.

One-dimensional characters may have worked in early films but today they couldn't be given away with hot tea. So Kent Walwin came up with the idea of a young man of the eighties, confronted with some of the perils that faced the Biggles of his own age back in 1917: a young man who was dragged into a hell-on-earth and asked to be a hero.

Walwin opened up the idea so that everyone could identify with it. He introduced the young American who participates in an untold Biggles story.

'What we are saying,' Walwin continues, 'is that Biggles

never told this story – except to Colonel Raymond. It never got into the books because it could seem rather stupid that he had been rescued in 1917 by an American who claimed to have come from 1985. 'Raymond, of course, followed the story through to the moment in 1985 on the exact "time" anniversary, when he knocks on the door of the young American and asks if he is all right.' This provides the start to the new adventure.

Walwin decided to counterpoint the heroics of then and the heroics of now which would allow a number of acceptable things to be done without 'modernising' Biggles and which would have lost what he was – a hero.

Walwin explains that Biggles' commanding officer, Colonel Raymond – played by Peter Cushing – is equivalent to the 'M' character in Bond, but is also the present-day link with the Biggles of the past. Biggles and Co were nearly always sent on a mission by Colonel Raymond, and Walwin felt that Peter Cushing was absolutely ideal to play the part: he had to have clarity of look, but also be an old man back in business!

GETTING BIGGLES OFF THE GROUND

At last!

Those two words not only echo the satisfaction among the team responsible for bringing BIGGLES to the cinema screen, but also the anticipation among the countless millions who have read so many of the BIGGLES books and waited so patiently for their hero to take off from the pages and on to the silver screen. He has been such an obvious candidate as a 'film hero' that it is surprising it has not happened before.

It has to be said that it is not for want of trying. But although there have been many hurdles along the way since Kent Walwin first came to the project back in 1975, BIGGLES finally made it and once more got off the ground! This time in a superb new adventure, with a modern – and sometimes amazing – ingredient which leaves Biggles, the much admired hero, intact.

Yellowbill, the production company, was formed in 1975, and one of its first achievements was to buy the rights to Biggles. The original idea came from one of the then active directors, Peter James. He and Walwin were the two main founding directors of the company and were looking for projects which could be developed. They wanted to do something that was very British, and felt that Bond had probably been the only really British subject that had longevity and could continue to be churned out. But Bond wasn't owned by the British, so Yellowbill thought it would have a go at Biggles.

'Biggles has similarities to Bond,' says Walwin. 'He is the ultimate hero. Bond was less experienced than Biggles, however. Bond has only X-number of books, and Biggles had ninety-seven. Biggles had survived more, seen more, had less women than Bond; Biggles probably kept his eye on the job more than the flesh. We thought he was a good idea.'

Yellowbill was a spin-off from a Canadian group which Walwin and Peter James were part-founders of in the late '60s. They made about fifteen features by the time they eventually split away from Canada in 1978. But in 1975 they were the British division of a Canadian company which they controlled.

One of the assets was Biggles. It took quite a long time to clear all the books, and it wasn't until about 1977 that Yellowbill knew what they owned: there had been all ninety-seven books on which they had to clear the copyrights. Then they started to look at what could be done with the character and embarked upon a screenplay which – had it been filmed today – would have cost an impossible thirty million dollars.

At this point Adrian Scrope (Executive Producer) joined the company, and a slice of it was sold to Foreign and Colonial, an investment management group who continues with Yellowbill to the present day. Yellowbill enlarged and from being a small development company it took on numerous interests and needed a larger producing partner.

A deal was struck with the Robert Stigwood Organisation in 1979, and although an enormous amount of work went into the development of the Biggles project it never got off the ground. Yellowbill had retained the option to buy the rights back and did so at the beginning of 1983. Biggles looked as if he would be put on ice but, says Walwin, 'Biggles won't be put down.'

Then a major public company expressed interest in giving Biggles a push: 'The company – a well-established City insurance brokers – was interested in providing a large part of the production finance. They would never have considered an investment of this size if it hadn't been BIGGLES. It was something which the board could understand. They knew we were not talking about porno movies, skin flicks, whatever. They knew it was going to be something that actually they would be quite proud to be associated with.'

That was at the beginning of 1984, and the brokers' lawyers spent an inordinate amount of time delving into the rights and making sure Yellowbill had everything they said they had – which they did. It was decided that, because of changing tax legislation in the UK, filming had to be completed by the end of March, 1985.

'So we had to take the enormous risk of actually starting pre-production before all the money had come in.' Scrope had to scurry around and find money to finance the pre-production. Again, BIGGLES came up trumps.

'If you are talking about Biggles, people will open doors for you and that's been proved over and over. Not only in the finance. When we were doing helicopter stunts over Tower Bridge we had to get Thames Water Authority, River Police, Tower Hamlets, City Corporation, everybody's approval. And because it was Biggles it really helped. I don't think we would ever have got the approval if it hadn't been for Biggles.'

'What is important,' Scrope asserts, 'for this first BIGGLES film is not to make an enormous amount of money out of it, but actually to have it seen by the widest possible audience. It was vitally important to get the North American release right. Although they are not aware of Biggles in that territory, neither were they aware of Indiana Jones before *Raiders of the Lost Ark* came out. So there was no disincentive. BIGGLES had to stand on its own. But the luxury they had was in being their own masters.

Scrope was delighted with the City involvement. 'They've blown hot and cold on it. But finally the film has been made, and finally the City is behind it, and I think that is something slightly worth waving the flag about,' he says. 'We want to do not only another Biggles, but other films, and we are showing the City that there is a role they can play without getting exposed to too much risk.' And he concludes: 'I think we are pretty well placed.'

As Kent Walwin says, 'by buying rights in a whole slew of books we foresaw the fact that we might be able to go on. We were looking for something with the quality of Bond, not just aesthetically in terms of what we could create, but financially. The subject lends itself to a mini-series – and there is almost certainly that somewhere down the line. And we could do another feature.

'What we are saying is that BIGGLES is our Bond. Bond is British, but we sold him lock, stock and barrel: he is owned by the Americans. I feel that within a country like ours, which is as much a melting-pot as America is, we have a lot of subject-matter. British characters are what I know. I was brought up on them. I think it's time we did our own. We should be proud of them.

'Biggles is one of the few British projects which is owned, financed and controlled lock, stock and barrel out of this country. And if it makes money, it will come back here and be ploughed back into production.'

Other Yellowbill dreams are well under way: the launch of a new television information magazine; working on Britain's first drive-in – Four M Four – which will be opened at exit four on the M4 close to London Airport, and which will cover sporting events. And there are the film and television projects.

But right now the focus is on BIGGLES. Perhaps getting the project off the ground has brought a sense of relief as well as a pride in achievement. Whatever the individual reaction from behind the camera, it is a certainty that audiences, internationally, will once more thrill to the adventures of a long-time hero on his latest and brand-new adventure.

CAPTAIN W. E. JOHNS – CREATOR OF BIGGLES

It would not be appropriate to discuss BIGGLES without reference to the author responsible for the huge number of books about the fabulous hero.

CAPTAIN W. E. JOHNS was born in 1893 in Hertford and educated at Hertford Grammar School. He had early ambitions to join the army, but his parents had other ideas and articled him to a local surveyor at sixteen. When the First World War broke out, he found himself enlisted with the Norfolk Yeomanry as Trooper Johns, serving first in the Middle East. After a period with the Machine Gun Cavalry Squadron in Salonica, he was commissioned, again in the Norfolk Yeomanry. Later, in 1916, he was seconded to the Royal Flying Corps. He served with 55 Squadron of the Independent Force, going first to France as a fighter-pilot and subsequently going out on two-seater bomber raids over Germany. During one of these, in September 1918, he was shot down over Mannheim by the famous German air ace Ernst Udet.

Wounded, he was taken prisoner and sentenced to death, but managed to escape. He was recaptured and sent to a punishment camp in Bavaria, where he remained until the end of the war. Johns enjoyed life in the RFC (later to become the RAF) and decided to stay. He served as a regular officer until 1930 when he was transferred to the Reserve, retaining his old RFC rank of Captain.

In 1930 he became Air Correspondent to several British

184

and overseas newspapers and magazines. His first book appeared in 1932 and was entitled FIGHTING PLANES AND ACES. Also in 1932 he became Founder-Editor of the monthly magazine, POPULAR FLYING; it was in the pages of this magazine that Biggles made his debut in a series of short stories. The first story was called THE WHITE FOKKER and was succeeded by many more short flying stories featuring Biggles. The first collection of THE CAMELS ARE COMING was published in 1932, and was followed by several more. Then the full-length Biggles books started to flow, one of the earliest being BIGGLES LEARNS TO FLY (1935) showing the hero at the start of his illustrious career.

Since then ninety-seven Biggles books have been published. Biggles was given a new lease of life after the Second World War when he was seconded to the powerful Interpol as an Air Detective. Several million copies a year are sold in seventeen different countries.

During the Second World War, Johns toured all over Britain lecturing for the RAF. During this period two more well-known fictional characters were created by Johns – Worrals of the WAAF. and Gimlet, the Commando. He introduced them at the suggestion of the Air Ministry and the War Office respectively, who each wanted to speed up recruiting, and wrote a series of books about them. He wrote around two hundred books altogether including several non-fiction titles such as THE AIR VC's (1934) and MILESTONES OF AVIATION (1935). He also wrote a series of science-fiction books for boys.

Captain Johns died in 1968.

To play the part of Biggles, the producers selected NEIL DICKSON, a young and talented actor who brilliantly and visually measures up to the established image of Biggles. During production there were frequent remarks from crew, actors and visitors to the set that Neil Dickson 'looked exactly like Biggles'. This was no idle flattery: it was clear endorsement of the very real need for the actor to match the image. If it was wrong the whole concept could be lost.

From being a boxing champion at school and going on to the Guildhall School of Drama, NEIL DICKSON moved through weekly rep into the West End theatre and then did a lot of television work. Theatre continued to dominate his career, however, and one of his most satisfactory roles to date was in 'Trafford Tanzi' at London's Mermaid Theatre, in which he played the part of a wrestler. Most recently he played a major role in 'Anno Domini', which has yet to reach the television screens.

Cast in the role of the young American who is transported into the World War I trenches is ALEX HYDE WHITE, the young actor son of the highly regarded character actor, Wilfred Hyde White. Although Alex has appeared in numerous television productions, including 'Hill Street Blues', 'Quincy' and 'Voyagers' among them, and appeared in two feature films, 'The Toy' and 'The First Olympics – Athens 1896', he regards BIGGLES as his big break.

Although his is not the title role the script provides him with a very strong part and he feels he would have to go a very long way to find a character that is as heroic and as strong.

'After seven years in the business,' he says, 'anything I have done before this means nothing to me, except for the fact that it has trained me. It is work one does not have to get, and if you do, it makes you feel good. Movies are what I wanted to do, it's what I always wanted to do, and I always felt I could.'

FIONA HUTCHISON plays the young American woman caught up in the adventures which befall her fiancé and business partner. Fiona makes her feature film debut in BIGGLES following a career in ballet which commenced at the age of five. She trained with the Royal Ballet before moving to New York City School of American Ballet and then to the American Ballet Theatre. An accident which damaged her back prevented full development of a career in ballet and she worked briefly and successfully in commercials before securing the part in BIGGLES.

PETER CUSHING brings to his role of Colonel Raymond the stature which has marked his enormously successful career in films, theatre and television. So many outstanding titles feature among his vast list of credits which extend back to his first film, 'Man in the Iron Mask', made in 1939; 'Love From a Stranger', the first title among his theatre credits and which started in 1940; and back to 1951 and 'Eden End' which commenced his extensive work in television.

Peter Cushing still gets an enormous thrill out of his work, 'I love it,' he says. 'But I am still amazed, even after all these years, that I am offered work. During the lean years I never thought the 'phone would ring. And every time I get a call – even now – I think, "How lovely, someone still wants me." The only thing I find, the more I do, the more difficult I find it because I think there is much more responsibility placed upon one's shoulders; the audience expects so much of someone they have seen for so many years. You feel you can't always give what you would like to, though I suppose one does. I always feel "I wish that was a rehearsal, now let's do it!"'

Biggles, says Cushing, is more his cup of tea than 007, '007 is marvellous, but he is so invulnerable, whereas Biggles is so vulnerable: he survives, but there is the possibility he won't.

'I have a feeling that BIGGLES will do for its young men what "Star Wars" did for its principals: they all made it big.'

Chuck Dinsmore is played by WILLIAM HOOTKINS. Chuck is the ever-eating, woman-loving bulky friend and business associate of American Jim Ferguson. For a young actor Hootkins has a considerable number of credits behind him; among them: 'Raiders of the Lost Ark', 'Bad Timing', and 'Star Wars', numerous television and stage credits and recent work which includes the features 'Trail of the Pink Panther', 'Water' and 'White Nights'; 'Bergerac' and 'Private Eye' for television; and London stage roles including 'The Dentist' and 'The Watergate Tapes' at the Royal Court. His stage performances also include Churchill in 'What a Way to Run a Revolution' and Hercule Poiret in 'Peril at End House'.

Jim Ferguson's other colleague, Bill Kizitski, is played by the young actor ALAN POLONSKY, who has a wide range of feature film credits, television roles and theatre credits. He trained at the Guildhall School of Music and Drama following a childhood dream of becoming an actor and which began when his parents started taking him to the Old Vic and the Aldwych to see the National Theatre and Royal Shakespeare Company.

'I wanted to be up there doing,' he says, and has never lost his enthusiasm for the theatre. 1985 started off well for him and his part in BIGGLES continued that good start. He hopes his career will eventually enable him to work on both sides of the Atlantic and is glad to be seen in a film where he is playing a significant part which will be seen in the States and which gives him a certain amount of credibility.

Biggles, as his many fans would quickly point out, has the unstinting support of three close friends: Bertie, Algy and Ginger.

JAMES SAXON, who plays Bertie, had images of how Biggles would be, although he had never actually read any of the books. On being cast in the role of Bertie he did his homework and found that the character was not as foolish as he had thought him to be.

Saxon wanted to get the character right and enjoyed the action offered by the role as opposed to the roles he was more used to playing in which he sits about in smoking jackets in chairs. In BIGGLES he is toting guns!

James Saxon's background is both on stage and in television. He appeared in 'We'll Meet Again' as an American flyer, and most recently appeared in the series 'Brass' on television.

MICHAEL SIBERRY, who plays the somewhat elegant and aristocratic Algy, makes his feature film debut in the role. He will be remembered for his recent performance in 'Hay Fever' for BBC television, in which he played Simon Bliss.

Among his numerous other credits for stage and television are the co-lead in 'Sherlock Holmes' for Granada TV, 'Strangers and Brothers' and 'Old Men at the Zoo' for the BBC, 'La Ronde', 'Richard II', 'Hamlet', 'The Merchant of Venice' and 'Romeo and Juliet' with the Royal Shakespeare Company. On tour and at the Haymarket Theatre he played Yasha in 'The Cherry Orchard' directed by Lindsay Anderson. He also enjoyed great success playing Jimmy Winter in 'Oh Kay' at the Chichester Festival.

For DANIEL FLYNN the part of Ginger gives him his first film work. Previously he has enjoyed a mixture of television and theatre roles which followed his training at RADA. He completed his training in August 1982 and quickly secured parts in 'No Excuses' for Central Television and 'Two Gentlemen of Verona' and 'Goodbye Mr Chips' for the BBC.

MARCUS GILBERT is cast in BIGGLES as the German Captain von Stalhein and – as seems fitting for the fighting character he portrays – includes among his accomplishments, riding, driving, motorbiking, stage-fighting, squash, archery, shooting, swimming, singing bass baritone and athletics!

Von Stalhein himself might be hard-pressed to provide such a list. Marcus Gilbert includes 'Master of the Game',

'The Last Days of Pompeii' and 'The Mask of Death' among his feature film credits, as well as numerous plays for television and several theatre productions.

There are those who may not recall the lady in Biggles' life. She fell in love with him and double-crossed her own side in order to save his life. But the course of true love never did run smooth and Marie – for the purpose of this production – is now living with an order of Belgian nuns. However, she is still able to provide Biggles with information and a map which helps him in his search for the secret weapon.

The part of Marie is played by FRANCESCA GONSHAW who has appeared in many television series since she completed her training at drama school. Notably she has appeared in ''Allo, 'Allo' for the BBC, 'The Hound of the Baskervilles' and in 'Shades' in the BBC's Play for Tomorrow series.

Director, JOHN HOUGH, came to BIGGLES following the classic telephone call 'straight out of the blue'. He had heard BIGGLES had been in preparation for some years and had dismissed it from his mind. Then came the telephone call to meet the producers.

John Hough had visions of BIGGLES being the traditional character he had read about as a boy. But when he met Kent Walwin and Pom Oliver (the producers) and was presented with Kent's concept, he found it 'so bizarre, so strange and unreal', that he immediately wanted to do it. 'And somehow it made sense that I did it because of my background of doing films and shows that are bizarre and fantasy,' he says.

That background included, to date, directing twelve feature films plus many television shows and series. He featured in the BBC2 programme 'Man Alive' as Britain's most promising film director. Four of his films feature in the all-time box-office championship list and include 'Dirty Mary – Crazy Larry', 'Witch Mountain' and 'Hell House'.

Most recently he has directed 'The Black Arrow' for Disney.

The story of Biggles stretches back more than ten years. Producer, Kent Walwin explains that the production company, Yellowbill, was formed as a development company back in 1975 and began looking for projects and one of its first tasks was to buy the rights to BIGGLES. The idea for the project had been sparked because the Yellowbill team felt that to date, 'Bond' was probably the only really British film that had longevity and which could carry on being churned out. And that wasn't owned by the British.

'There have been a few British "flashes in the pan",' explains Walwin, 'but nothing that was a long-term project. We thought we should have a go at Biggles because he had similarities to Bond. Biggles is the ultimate hero. Bond was less experienced: he had only a small number of books compared to Biggles, with ninety-seven. Biggles had survived more, seen more had less women than Bond and probably kept his eye on the job more than the flesh. We thought Biggles was a good idea.'

It took a long time to clear the rights on all the books and it wasn't until 1977 that Yellowbill knew what it owned. Then a screenplay was developed which, if it had been filmed today would have cost an impossible thirty million dollars.

Meanwhile, Yellowbill was growing up and a major slice of the company was sold to an investment management group, Foreign and Colonial. The company enlarged, there were more directors and more resources. Kent Walwin was left to develop other projects within the Yellowbill Group while a larger producing partner was sought.

Eventually a deal was struck with the Robert Stigwood Organisation in 1979, and there was enormous hard work to get the Biggles project off the ground with a lot of money being put into its development. But the film didn't get made; the Stigwood operation contracted in this country, and under the terms of Yellowbill's agreement, they had the right to buy the project back at the end of 1983.

Yellowbill exercised its rights and planned to put the project temporarily on ice. But Biggles wouldn't be put down or frozen!

At this stage a major public company, who already did business with Yellowbill, said they would be very interested in giving Biggles a big push. They came in as the main financiers of the film and, with Yellowbill's other corporate shareholders, made possible the 100 per cent British financed production.

BIGGLES had taken off!